"You Don't Make Things Easy, McGregor,"

Nolan rasped.

"I didn't create this situation, Lieutenant. I came here and *volunteered* my services. I didn't have to do that. And I don't have to stand here and take crap from you, either. Now, you either let me fly this bird, or I'm going through the chain of command to get your butt put in a sling so high you'll never see the ground again."

Nolan stood there, clenching his teeth. Anger and frustration warred in him. No, he didn't want his career going down the tubes over this. It wasn't worth it. Rubbing his chin, he studied Rhona. Damn, she was beautiful. Too bad she was his copilot. Otherwise, he could think of other more pleasurable ways of spending time with her.

"Okay," he growled, "you win this round, McGregor. Now, get your butt over to Supply. This bird is ready to go...."

Dear Reader,

Welcome to Silhouette Desire! This month we've created a brand-new lineup of passionate, powerful and provocative love stories just for you.

Begin your reading enjoyment with *Ride the Thunder* by Lindsay McKenna, the September MAN OF THE MONTH and the second book in this beloved author's cross-line series, MORGAN'S MERCENARIES: ULTIMATE RESCUE. An amnesiac husband recovers his memory and returns to his wife and child in *The Secret Baby Bond* by Cindy Gerard, the ninth title in our compelling DYNASTIES: THE CONNELLYS continuity series.

Watch a feisty beauty fall for a wealthy lawman in *The Sheriff & the Amnesiac* by Ryanne Corey. Then meet the next generation of MacAllisters in *Plain Jane MacAllister* by Joan Elliott Pickart, the newest title in THE BABY BET: MacALLISTER'S GIFTS.

A night of passion leads to a marriage of convenience between a gutsy heiress and a macho rodeo cowboy in *Expecting Brand's Baby*, by debut Desire author Emilie Rose. And in Katherine Garbera's new title, *The Tycoon's Lady* falls off the stage into his arms at a bachelorette auction, as part of our popular BRIDAL BID theme promotion.

Savor all six of these sensational new romances from Silhouette Desire today.

Enjoy!

Joan Marlow Golan

Joan Marlow Golan
Senior Editor, Silhouette Desire

Please address questions and book requests to:
Silhouette Reader Service
U.S.: 3010 Walden Ave., P.O. Box 1325, Buffalo, NY 14269
Canadian: P.O. Box 609, Fort Erie, Ont. L2A 5X3

Lindsay
McKenna
RIDE THE THUNDER

Published by Silhouette Books
America's Publisher of Contemporary Romance

SILHOUETTE BOOKS

ISBN 0-373-76459-6

RIDE THE THUNDER

This edition published by arrangement with Harlequin Books S.A.

® and TM are trademarks of Harlequin Books S.A., used under license.
Trademarks indicated with ® are registered in the United States Patent
and Trademark Office, the Canadian Trade Marks Office and in other
countries.

Visit Silhouette at www.eHarlequin.com

Printed in U.S.A.

Books by Lindsay McKenna

LINDSAY McKENNA

A homeopathic educator, Lindsay teaches at the Desert Institute of Classical Homeopathy in Phoenix, Arizona. When she isn't teaching alternative medicine, she is writing books about love. She feels love is the single greatest healer in the world and hopes that her books touch her readers on those levels.

To Barbara Ward and Judy Coldicott of Dunedin,
New Zealand, who surely ride the thunderbolts of life.
As homeopaths willing to step into uncharted waters
to increase your knowledge of healing, you are
true heroines. I'm proud to be your friend.

One

Lieutenant Nolan Galway decided he was having a bad hair day. Actually, it was a lot worse than that. As he strode toward the Operations building at Camp Reed, the noise of helicopters and jets landing and taking off in the late afternoon hammered at his ears. Tuning out the earsplitting sounds, he tried to focus on one thing only: getting a new copilot.

As he approached the Ops building which was made of gray concrete and looked like a rectangular box with a tower sticking up at one end, he saw that it was a regular Grand Central Station today, just as it had been ever since the killer earthquake hit on New Year's Eve. From the moment that quake struck, Nolan's life and everyone else's in the surrounding southern Los Angeles area had been turned into pure chaos.

He tried to keep his stride steady, but his heart was pounding and his adrenaline pumping. He *wanted* a copilot, he decided with new resolve. The OOD—officer of the day—could ground him without one. If he didn't have a copilot, Nolan couldn't fly his critical missions and save people's lives. Somehow, somewhere, he had to find a replacement for his former partner, who had nearly died of food poisoning this morning on the flight back from the quake-damaged region of Southern California.

The plight of the people in the devastated Los Angeles basin tugged at Nolan's heart and soul. Though the President of the United States had already declared California a major disaster area and FEMA was coming to help too, there were depot centers being set up around the U.S. to take food, medicine and blankets. But until roads were created to take more supplies, they remained at the centers. All available helicopters were being used to fly them to the basin. People were dying because they couldn't get enough helicopter flights in to provide much-needed water and food.

"Dammit," he mumbled, thinning his lips. Ops was alive with activity. As he rounded the corner, cutting across a stretch of yellowed Bermuda grass, and headed for the front door where the OOD was standing watch, his focus was momentarily drawn from his tactical objective.

Coming out of the bright sunlight and heading for Ops with the same resolve and determination that he felt was a woman. What made Nolan take notice was the fact that, of the hundred or so marines and navy personnel running about the place, she was the only person in civilian clothes. Everyone else wore dark navy uniforms or the desert camouflage of marines.

Rubbing his face briskly to stave off his exhaustion, Nolan saw that she was tall, and that her long black hair swayed with each stride she took. She wore slacks and a jacket to keep away the chill of the January day yet he could see her feminine curves. Though it was silly under the circumstances, he was immediately drawn to her.

Hesitating momentarily, Nolan found himself wanting to slow his speed and intersect her path. There was no earthly reason why he should do that, of course. The sidewalk was crowded with people coming and going, their faces grim. The urgent task before all of them at this Marine Corps base was to try and save the lives of millions of innocent people, and here he was, caught up over a woman.

Maybe he was sleep deprived to the point of no return, Nolan thought as he halted on the sidewalk. During the past week, he and his copilot had been flying dawn to dusk, never getting more than five hours sleep at one stretch. Now, as he stood in place, people flowed around him as if he were a rock in a wildly rushing river. A river of humans hurrying to their duty stations to load supplies of food, water and medicine on the awaiting helos nearby.

His eyes narrowed on the woman as she approached. Nolan liked the way her hair, loose and

thick about her shoulders, swung in graceful time with
her swift gait. Just the way she walked told him she
was military. Her shoulders were thrown back proudly,
and her posture was erect and confident. Her eyes, he
noticed as she came closer, were fixed on the Ops
doors.

"Can I help you?" he asked. "You look like you're
hunting for someone or something."

Her gaze snapped from the doors to him.

Wearing his beaten up, old leather bombardier
jacket, a white scarf around his neck to prevent chafing
from his dark green, one-piece fight uniform, Nolan
stood with his hands relaxed on his hips. He gave her
a slight smile.

She had gray eyes. Soft, warm, rabbit-fur gray. Yet
there was something of the eagle in the way she
looked up at him. Her eyes thawed and widened
slightly as his own gaze took in her dusty jeans, which
showed her long, slender legs. She was also wearing
leather hiking boots, and a dark blue knapsack on her
back.

"Why…yes, I'm looking for the Logistics building." She gestured toward the building behind him
and tried to catch her breath. "I know this is Ops. I
was hoping—"

"Over there," Nolan said brusquely, lifting his
hand and pointing. "That three-story, dark green
building up on the hill. That's Logistics."

She was breathing hard, as if she'd been running.
From the knees down, her jeans were very dusty, and
as he looked more closely, Nolan saw beads of per-

spiration on her furrowed brow. Several tendrils of that thick, bluish-black hair stuck to her temples. Where had she come from? Why had she been running like that? And why was she so dusty? Nolan had plenty of questions about this compelling stranger.

He watched as she twisted to look where he was pointing. Her hair once again swung gently, like a black cap, about her shoulders. She was attractive and arresting; not a raving beauty, but that didn't matter. Nolan liked her face, especially her alert, large gray eyes.

"Phew. Great. Thanks..." And she turned on her heel and began to trot back toward the hill.

"Hi, my name is...and what's yours?" Nolan murmured wryly to himself, unsure whether to be upset with her rude departure or not. Scratching his head, he grinned slightly. "I guess she's in a helluva hurry, Nolan. Come on, son, you have other fish to fry...like rustlin' up a new copilot...." And he headed up the concrete steps of Ops to do battle with the OOD. If only the officer could find him a copilot!

Still, as he reached the top, the chill of the early-evening air making him shiver slightly, Nolan smiled to himself. Who the hell was that woman? Not that he should be interested. Still, he liked her high cheekbones and those soft gray eyes of hers. He wondered what her name was, then decided that his musing had no place on his roster for the day. He was a pilot in search of a partner. Nothing else could matter at the moment.

* * *

January 7: 1615

"You need me!"

Morgan Trayhern halted instantly as the woman's strident cry rang throughout the passageway where he'd been walking. Scowling, he turned around, a sheaf of papers in his hand. At the other end of the hall, where two marine guards were posted, a tall, slim woman stood. Her hair, an ebony color with blue highlights, hung around her proud shoulders. Everything about her shouted patrician, from her oval face to her fine, thin Roman nose, high cheekbones and narrowed gray eyes. The look on her face was one of pure frustration as she stood, her hands set defiantly on her hips, confronting the tense sentries. The OOD, Lieutenant Ted Monroe, stood behind the two sentries. He was a shavetail lieutenant, having just recently joined the corps. His square face was as purple as a plum and his large hands were set arrogantly on his own hips. The two guards had their rifles up across their chests, as if warning the woman not to come a step closer, Morgan noted.

The air seemed to snap and shiver with tension. The whole base was immersed in the earthquake disaster planning, in the wake of the 8.9 quake that had hit the Los Angeles basin area a week ago. Everyone was in a state of high stress, including, obviously, the three marines.

Frowning, Morgan looked closely at the woman, and decided she looked familiar. Turning, he headed back to where the confrontation was taking place. As he neared the standoff, his lips tugged into a grin.

"Rhona McGregor!" he thundered, his face breaking into an effusive smile. Morgan stopped beside the flustered young OOD officer. "Ted, this is an old friend of mine. Relax. Let her pass. She's one of us, okay?"

Immediately contrite, the officer blinked and then barked at his two tense sentries, "At ease!"

Rhona sighed and stared across the line of demarcation at Morgan. "I never expected to find you here, Morgan." She thrust out her long, thin hand in his direction, then smiled kindly at the embarrassed officer and sentries, who stepped aside.

Gripping her hand, Morgan said, "How are you, Rhona? And what on earth are you doing *here?* Last time Laura and I saw you was at your cousin, Paige Black's, wedding to Thane Hamilton in Arizona."

The warmth and firm strength of Morgan's hand made her travails of the last two days worth it. "Yes, that's right." She smiled briefly. "I was lucky to be able to wrangle some leave from the navy to be there for my cousin's wedding. Speaking of family, how's Laura?"

Grimacing, Morgan released Rhona's hand. He looked down the passageway milling with people. "She's here with me. Let's take a minute and chat. My makeshift office is right over here." He flashed Rhona a smile. "It's mine temporarily—for the duration of this disaster relief phase we're in."

Following him into the small cubicle, Rhona sighed.

She saw a pitcher of ice water and some glasses on a walnut sideboard. "Mind if I help myself? I'm a little footsore and thirsty."

"No, go ahead," Morgan murmured as he shut the door. Looking her up and down, he was struck by how long and lean she was. Though her mother was Navajo, Rhona looked decidedly more white than Native American, despite her dark hair and high cheekbones. Maybe she took after her dad, a doctor on the res in Arizona, Morgan mused. With a name like McGregor he must be of Scottish extraction. Thoughtfully, Morgan noted her dusty jeans, nicked and scarred hiking boots, and beat-up blue knapsack that had U.S. Navy written on the back in gold letters.

Once the cool water sated her thirst, Rhona set the glass down on the sideboard and turned back to the desk where Morgan was sitting. He was frowning at some reports in his hand. Taking a chair, she pulled it to the center of the room, in front of his desk.

"A lot has happened since I saw you and Laura last. For one thing, I resigned my navy commission six months ago."

"What?" Morgan lifted his head and devoted all his attention to the young woman before him. He liked her solid confidence and steadiness. But then, she was a trained combat helicopter pilot and needed that kind of demeanor.

Shrugging, Rhona muttered, "I got tired of knocking elbows with the Neanderthal guys of my squadron, Morgan. It was pure sexual harassment, and I wasn't into giving my power and time away to them or the navy anymore. The higher-ups in my squadron were still lookin' the other way even after Tailhook. I tried to get a transfer to another helo squadron, where half the pilots are women and I'd have some camaraderie, but it was a no go.''

"I see," he said sadly. "They've lost a helluva good pilot."

"Thanks," Rhona said. She brightened. "But life goes on, doesn't it? You know, since I'm part Navajo, I have a strong environmental ethic in me. So I decided to start my own crop-dusting business here in Southern California. I got a loan to buy a helicopter, and the rest is history. The big difference is that I'm not using damaging pesticides." She grinned. "I did some research and found out neem oil, from a tree in India, is a natural pesticide. So I spray crops with it."

"Fascinating. Does it work as well as a commercial pesticide?"

"Yep. And it's environmentally safe for all concerned. Keeps the pests off the plants, it's biodegradable, plus safe for Mom Earth." Rhona opened her hands. "I had the best of all worlds going for me until this earthquake hit."

"Didn't we all," Morgan murmured. He frowned. "You look worn-out. What have you been doing? Walking? There're no highways left to drive on."

"No kidding. I live over in Bonsall, which is about twenty miles from Camp Reed. When the quake hit, there wasn't much I could do where I was. I figured that, since I'm very recently out of the navy, and am still qualified to fly a military helicopter, you might need my services here at the base." Leaning forward, her voice filled with excitement, she said, "Morgan, I've come to volunteer to help fly in supplies. I know that Camp Reed is probably the only base up and running in the Los Angeles basin right now."

"You're right about that. We're *it*. No land vehicles can get anywhere near the epicenter of the quake, which is located in south L.A. Right now, we're limited to helicopters ferrying food, water and medicine, or transporting those who need surgery to this hospital. We've got C-141 Starlifters bringing everything we need in to this airport, and taking some of the injured out to a hospital in Seattle."

"Yes, I saw a couple of Starlifters being unloaded on the apron," Rhona murmured. "This airport is overwhelmed with traffic, both rotocraft and fixed wing."

"Yes, we are."

"I figured the pilots stationed here are about worn-out and you could use some fresh replacements. I'm volunteering to do that." Rhona leaned forward, her voice low with concern. "I'm qualified to fly the UH-1N Huey, and the CH-46E Sea Knight, Morgan. I see they have both models down at the airport. Are you in a position here at the base to get me slotted as a relief pilot in either of them? I'll go wherever you need me. I'd use my own chopper but it has been retrofitted for crop dusting. I left it tethered at my airport." She smiled a little. "A pilot is a pilot, right?"

Morgan felt a wave of warmth move through him. How like Rhona to volunteer. She was a good, strong woman who had an enduring work ethic and sense of community. "I think your Navajo blood is showing," he stated in a husky tone. "This community is reeling from this earthquake and you're pitching in. You could have stayed in Bonsall and fought for your own survival."

Shrugging, Rhona grinned. "Not me. I like being where the action is, Morgan. You know that. I might be a civilian now, but you can't take the military out of my blood." She saw Morgan's blue eyes gleam approvingly. He picked up his pen and studied her thoughtfully.

"Sure you wouldn't like to close up your crop-dusting business and come work for me? I can use someone with your patriotism and moxie."

Laughing, Rhona shook her head. "Nah. Thanks, though, Morgan. I love to fly. I love Mom Earth. Being a crop duster and helping out with the food we put in our mouths makes me feel good. I guess I'm more Indian than I ever thought."

"Just because you don't live on the res doesn't lessen your ties with your people," he said.

"That's true," Rhona murmured. "My parents supported my decision to leave the navy. I had many talks with both of them. My mother, who is full blood, thought turning my energies and focus toward helping the earth was a far better use of my time." Rhona grinned.

Rummaging through a pile of papers teetering on his crowded desk, Morgan said, "Your mother's right. It's the navy's loss, though…. I've got the flight

schedules here. Let me look through them." He
scowled and ran his index finger down the pilot roster.
"Ah…here we go. Lieutenant Nolan Galway just lost
his copilot to a bad case of food poisoning…." Morgan lifted his head. "With no electricity except here
on base, we're learning that the box lunches we're
making in the chow hall need better refrigeration. We
had four pilots go down. Nolan's copilot was just
taken out by Starlifter to Seattle. He had a dangerous
kind of food poisoning. If it's not nailed with antibi-
otics, it could stop his kidneys from functioning."

Shaking her head, Rhona murmured, "There're all
kinds of things out there that can bite us in the butt if
we can't keep foodstuffs properly refrigerated." She
patted her well-worn navy knapsack. "I walked
twenty miles today and ate nothing but some granola
bars. They're a safe bet because they don't need refrigeration."

"Wise woman," Morgan replied. "Yeah, we're
overwhelmed here. Our refrigeration units are
crammed, and with more planes and pilots coming and
going, and civilians pouring into the base for food,
water and medicine, we're running into food poisoning
more and more."

"So, you want me to partner up with Lieutenant
Galway? Stand in as his copilot and work his flight
schedule?"

"Yes, I do." Morgan picked up the phone. "Let
me contact Ops and get you officially on the roster."

"I've got proof of my flight proficiency and training

right here if you want to look at them.'' She patted her knapsack, which rested on her lap.

Shaking his head, Morgan punched in the number for the flight desk officer at Ops. ''Not necessary. I know you're qualified, Rhona.''

Her heart beat a little harder. Looking around the small, spare green office, Rhona realized she had missed life in the military, after all. Well, maybe some of it. What she didn't miss were the Neanderthal males who thought women pilots weren't their equals. Her hearing keyed on Morgan's deep voice as he spoke to a Major Hickman, who was apparently the commanding officer of the pilot roster judging by the discussion Morgan was having with him. Smiling to herself, Rhona decided Morgan could charm a dead person back to life, he had such a persuasive gift of gab. Not many people had it. At Thane and Paige's wedding, Rhona had been entranced by Morgan and his blond-haired wife, Laura. They were such a loving couple. What was nice was they'd been married for a long time and were obviously still in love and happy with one another.

Sighing internally, Rhona realized that would never happen for her. The look in Laura's eyes as she'd gazed adoringly up at Morgan during the ceremony was something Rhona kept in her heart of hearts. Wouldn't it be nice to have a man adore her, love her, in the same way?

Hearing Morgan hang up, Rhona lifted her chin and looked at him. He seemed pleased.

"You're in," Morgan said. "Major Hickman is jumping up and down for joy."

"He knows I'm a woman?"

"Yes, and he didn't bat an eyelash over it. In his book—and he's the head of the flight desk operations over there—you're a warm body who knows how to fly a chopper. He doesn't give one whit about your gender."

"Great!"

Morgan frowned. "You've got to be hungry. Twenty miles you walked? That's a helluva hike, Rhona. You look a little tired, too."

Shrugging her thin shoulders, Rhona murmured, "Listen, growing up on the res and running after a flock of sheep, I could put in twenty miles a day keeping up with them as they foraged for grass on that red desert."

"Still," Morgan said, standing, "I told Major Hickman you'd see him in about two hours. You need to get some food in your stomach." Brightening as he came around the desk, he asked, "Were you able to let your parents know you're okay? I'm sure they're worried sick about you since Bonsall is south of the epicenter of the quake."

Rising, Rhona murmured, "Yes, I have a cell phone." She patted the leather case on her belt. "I got ahold of Paige in Sedona. There're no cell phones up on the res, so I called her and asked her to contact my parents the old-fashioned way—via a real live telephone."

Chuckling, he slid his arm through hers and guided

her toward the door. "Good. I'm sure they're resting easier knowing you're safe. Come on, I'm going to take you to see Laura. She's up at the hospital recovering from ankle surgery. I'll order in a tray of food for you while you two chat and catch up with one another."

"Laura's hurt?"

"Yeah," Morgan said wryly. "We were out here celebrating New Year's at a hotel when the quake hit. Luckily, a marine search team—a woman and her dog—found Laura under the rubble. I'd escaped because I was down at the bar having a drink with an old friend. I ran out of the hotel before it collapsed, but Laura wasn't so lucky. But thank God they found her and got her out of there. A marine helicopter flew us here, and while she was preparing for surgery, I volunteered myself to Logistics. Laura is recovering well, but she's confined to the hospital for now. While she's there she's taking care of a baby girl they found in the rubble near the hotel. The mother died, unfortunately, but Laura is helping out the nurses on the Obstetrics floor by feeding the baby and keeping her warm and safe in her arms." He smiled fondly. "Laura loves babies. Besides, it's keeping her busy and keeping her mind off the fact that her leg is hoisted up on weights and she can't go anywhere. You know how active she always is? Well, this staying in bed twenty-four hours a day is wearing on her. Taking care of the little girl is a healthy diversion for her."

Rhona opened the office door. "Gosh, what a story,

Morgan! You two always seem to be where the action is.''

Once out in the busy passageway, Morgan dropped his hand from her arm. She followed him down to the end of the corridor, where he pushed open the door. It was near dusk, about 1700, or 5:00 p.m. The sun was setting, the sky a blood-red color. That symbol wasn't lost on Rhona. Her Indian heritage had taught her to read nature as a reflection of humankind. And right now, Los Angeles was hemorrhaging, as thousands of people lay dead or dying. Just the thought dampened her spirits.

Morgan led her down another crowded passageway. ''Believe me, this was one time that Laura and I weren't looking for any action at all. I'd planned this little getaway for us some time ago, as a Christmas surprise for her.'' Shaking his head as he opened the outer door and held it for Rhona, he muttered, ''And here we thought we'd enjoy a nice, quiet five days away from my office and her demands, and just enjoy one another....''

Rhona followed him down the metal-grate stairs to the lawn below. Although night was approaching rapidly, and the lights were on, Camp Reed was a beehive of nonstop activity. As they left the Logistics building, she could see the airport, and all the helicopters coming and going. She itched to get into the cockpit again and fly one of them. Watching her step, she hurried beside Morgan along a cracked sidewalk toward the hospital, which was about a quarter of a mile away.

Rhona was in awe at how busy the whole place was.

The airport was obviously too small for all the airplanes and helicopters that were crowding in there, bringing in lifesaving foodstuffs and medical help. The pilots must be exhausted. They had to be. The quake had struck seven days ago, and now, as the ongoing emergency only grew worse, they had to be running on frayed nerves and sheer guts and determination to reach helpless people who desperately needed the supplies they flew in.

Hurrying to catch up with Morgan, Rhona carefully dodged jutting pieces of sidewalk shoved upward by the force of the quake. One wrong step and she'd trip and fall. Not that she hadn't on the way here. She had. Many times.

"I can hardly wait to see Laura!" she said enthusiastically as she finally came up beside him, eye-level with Morgan's broad shoulders.

"Laura is going to be overjoyed to see a familiar face," he assured her genially. "Right now, I try to drop in and see her for breakfast, lunch and dinner." Glancing at his watch, he said, "And we're right on time for dinner with her."

January 7: 1720

Rhona opened her arms and gave Laura a gentle, careful embrace of welcome. She saw the little baby nestled in a crib on the other side of the raised bed, so that Laura could pick up the pink-wrapped infant whenever she wanted.

Morgan ordered up three trays of food while the two women fussed over the sleeping infant.

"She's so cute," Rhona told Laura in a soft voice as she peeked into the crib at the sleeping infant. Glancing up, she asked "Do you have a name for her?"

Laura sighed and smiled. "No. Right now, she's officially known as 'baby Jane Fielding.' We know her mother's name was Fielding, but there was no identification on her body for her daughter."

Morgan came over and kissed his wife's cheek. "I just got word about possible relatives, honey."

Laura brightened. "Oh, good. What did you find out?"

"Well, checking on this is going very slowly because of the earthquake," he cautioned. "Priority is being given to the rescue efforts here in the L.A. basin. But I found out that the mother was adopted herself. The FBI has come to a dead end, and now they're searching for the mother's adoptive parents."

Rhona smiled softly at Laura. "I'm sorry the baby's mother died, but this little girl has the best of all worlds right now. She has you, Laura." Rhona looked at Morgan, who stood by his wife's bedside, his arm around her blue-gowned shoulders. "And you, Morgan. I wonder if you help change diapers?" She chuckled.

Giggling, Laura said, "Oh, yes, he does." She patted the box of diapers on the bedstand. "He's got lots of time in grade doing this for our own foursome over the years."

Just then an orderly in white wheeled in a cart with three dinner trays. He was small, with short-cropped blond hair and hazel eyes. His smile was infectious as he pulled up to Laura's bedside and said hello.

Rhona felt her stomach grumble. She realized how hungry she was. Nibbling on granola bars was okay, but when the orderly handed her an aluminum tray bearing a hamburger, steamed rice and broccoli, plus a dish of chocolate pudding, her mouth watered. Sitting down on a nearby chair, Rhona dove into the fare with gusto.

"Thanks, Morgan," she said between mouthfuls. "I'm starving!"

Laura settled her own tray over her lap and took the utensils Morgan handed her. "So, you're volunteering to fly here, Rhona? That's wonderful."

"Yes," Morgan said, making sure his wife was properly set up to eat before he settled down in a chair with his own tray. "And she walked twenty miles today from Bonsall to do it."

Eyes widening, Laura gave her a look of pure admiration. "That's a lotta miles, Rhona. Aren't you tired?"

"Yes, I am." Rhona looked toward the window, where the venetian blind was up so that they could see the airport. "But not as tired and exhausted as I know those pilots are."

"Well," Laura murmured, pride in her voice, "we're so lucky to have you here with us, Rhona. How many other people would do what you've done? Probably not many."

"It's my Indian blood," she murmured. "Indians are very conscientious about their community, and they pitch in to help when and where they can."

"I'm sure Lieutenant Nolan Galway is going to think you're an angel come from heaven," Morgan said. He put some ketchup on his hamburger, and then added mustard. "Right now, he can't fly without a copilot. That's a military rule. If something happened to him in the cockpit and he didn't have a copilot to take over, the chopper would be lost. So—" he grinned and picked up the hamburger "—I'm sure he's going to welcome you with open arms."

Rhona sighed. "I sure hope you're right, Morgan. But I'm a woman. Ex-navy. This guy is a marine, and you know how they feel about any other military service—like we're not worthy and all that macho bull."

Morgan eyed his chocolate pudding and decided to eat it next. "Hopefully, this guy isn't like the infamous Neanderthals you had the bad luck to be with in your squadron."

"Time will tell," Rhona murmured. As she continued to wolf down the hot, tasty food, she wondered about that. With a name like Galway, he had to be of Irish heritage. The fact that she was Scot and Navajo would make them mix like oil and water. Still, as she sat in the hospital room, with the sounds of helicopters and jet engines muffled by the brick walls, Rhona was excited. A part of her missed the military. Would this helicopter pilot be happy that she was now his partner and copilot? Rhona knew that in the coming weeks her life would not be her own. It would consist of flying the maximum hours allowed by aviation rules, dropping into exhausted sleep in a tent somewhere, and eating on the run as they jogged toward their cockpit. And all of it would be done with her partner, Lieutenant Nolan Galway. They'd do just about everything together—almost like being married, in a sense, because of the stresses and demands upon them to work as a close-knit team from dawn to dusk.

What would be his reaction to her? Rhona wasn't sure. In less than twelve hours, she'd find out.

Two

January 7: 1900

Of all things…! Nolan thought, turning and glaring at his Huey helicopter. It was dark and the garish lights from the flight line starkly illuminated ten Hueys, neatly parked nose to tail as they were loaded with another round of cargo destined for the L.A. basin.

Lieutenant Joyce Mason stood there with a roster in her hands, frowning at Nolan.

"I'm sorry, Lieutenant, but you can't take this Huey up to area six without a copilot. Your last temp, Lieutenant Steve Anselmo, was reassigned to his own Huey. You've got to stand down for tonight. Go back to the tent area and get some sleep. You've been flying for twelve hours nonstop today. Your copilot request has been logged. The major is seeing what can be done."

Harried, Nolan shoved his long fingers through his short, dark brown hair. He glared at the officer, and then at the men who were hurrying to load a cargo of bottled water into his chopper. "Look, gimme a break, will you, Joyce? You *know* there're people in my area that are literally dying of thirst. Would you deprive them?" He was in her face, glowering down at her as she stood before him in her dark green wool Marine Corps uniform and jacket to guard against the evening chill. Her cropped blond hair was tucked beneath her dark green garrison cap. Her eyes narrowed as he towered over her, trying to intimidate her into releasing him for one last flight.

"This won't work, Nolan. Stand down," she said, gritting her teeth. A slight wind riffled through the area and the papers on her clipboard rustled.

"Dammit, Joyce, I'm not intimidating you for the hell of it," he rasped, backing off. "Think about those people out there, will you?"

"I am," she said in a steely tone. "I'm thinking that you're sleep deprived, Nolan. You've had two temporary copilots, and you've used up both of their flying time allowance, while you've kept flying. Look at you!" She gestured toward his face. "You've got dark circles under your eyes. Your eyes are bloodshot. You're a cranky old bear, you're irritable and you're getting just plain mean. Now, this is an order—get out of here. Go to the chow hall and eat. Then go to the makeshift tent area and sleep, will you?"

Nolan knew he was beat. Joyce was from the flight desk. She didn't set the flight schedules, she only enforced them. Rubbing his jaw, which badly needed a shave, he looked around. The flight line reminded him of a harried hive of bees hyped up on an overdose of steroids. Ten huge tarpaulin-covered trucks had arrived, filled with medical, food and water supplies for the ten Hueys that were now on the flight line. Their blades were tied down, the pilots standing by or taking a quick break before they had to get to their assigned areas once again.

"Joyce," he said, exasperated, "you don't have another flight crew to take over my Huey. This bird is down until tomorrow morning, when you'll let me fly it again. What a waste! I could do one more flight. Just one?" And he held up a finger beseechingly.

Mouth tightening, Joyce said, "Nolan, I've known you almost two years now, and ordinarily, I'd let you get away with what you want. But not this time. You're tired. You've met your flight limit for a twenty-four-hour period. You don't have a co-pilot." She shook her head. "Somehow, I gotta find you one for tomorrow morning. They don't grow on trees, you know." Her own frustration was obvious in her soft voice. "Don't you think I want to give you clearance to deliver that water? Don't you think I know there're people out there, literally dying of thirst? I know area six is a Latino barrio, and it's really bad off, but I can't do this. I can't authorize it. I'd be looking at a court-martial, and I'm not willing to put my career on the line for it. Please…just go to the chow hall, grab something to eat and then go crash in your assigned tent.''

Nodding, Nolan whispered, ''Yeah, Joyce…I know you're right, but dammit, you don't see the hope in those little kids' faces when I land with food, medical or water supplies. You don't see the distraught look in the parents' eyes, either. Area six is hurting.'' He stepped forward. ''Can't you try and have the major swing a second Huey into area six? That barrio is elbow-to-elbow with families. Big families. They're starving to death out there, Joyce. Can you try and get a second flight of supplies in to them?''

She smiled grimly. ''You really know how to push my buttons, Galway. Heck, I can't even find you a copilot so you can fly tomorrow morning, and you're asking for a *second* flight with supplies into your area? You're dreaming. Get out of here. Go get some rest.''

Wearily, Nolan turned and looked unhappily at his bird, which was being refueled as three men from the truck carried box after box of bottled water into the rear cargo area. ''Damn,'' he muttered. Frustration tightened in his throat. He saw the darkness in Joyce's triangular face. ''Yeah…okay, Joyce. I hear you…but I don't like it….''

''I know,'' she said unhappily, coming up and patting him on the shoulder. ''Go on, Nolan. Get some well-earned rest. I'll see if I can pull any white rabbits out of a hat for you…but no promises, okay? We've lost three pilots to food poisoning in the last two days, and trying to get replacements in has been hell. You see how this airport is stacked up to the gum stumps with incoming and outgoing flights?''

Looking around, Nolan agreed. The huge C-141 Starlifters from the Air Force were bringing in record amounts of foodstuffs, which had to be transferred out of their wide, gaping bellies to awaiting military trucks. Once loaded, the trucks lumbered slowly, like elephants, over to the helicopter flight line. Ground crews then began loading the supplies onto the choppers. Once each helo was carrying a maximum weight load, it would take off to its assigned destination.

''Yeah…okay. Just find me a copilot, Joyce. I don't care if he's green and from Mars. Just so he can sit in the left-hand seat so I can legally fly my bird tomorrow morning, okay?''

Grinning tiredly, Joyce said, ''I even thought of blowing up one of those plastic balloon men and strapping it into your chopper so you could fly.''

Chuckling, Nolan said, ''You know where to find one?''

''Oh, no you don't!'' She laughed.

There wasn't much laughter around the airport and Nolan appreciated the moment with Joyce, who had one hell of a job assigning flights and juggling personnel to keep in compliance with Federal Aviation Agency rules of flying. They were desperate for more pilots. Everyone had met their maximum flight hours in the first seven days, and by now were exhausted. Push had come to shove, and Nolan knew they were in for a long haul. But he also knew that there were people out there beyond the base starving to death, dying from lack of water, or desperately needing emergency medical attention. The weight of that knowledge bore down on his broad shoulders like ten tons, and he couldn't escape it.

Again patting him on the back in a motherly fashion, Joyce murmured sympathetically, "Get out of here, Nolan. You've earned this rest."

"What time do you want me back here?"

"At 0500. But that's not a promise you can fly, or that I've found you a replacement copilot, okay? Don't come waltzin' in here like you're just gonna sit in that bird and take off. Come see me at the flight desk first."

"I hear you," he murmured, giving her a wink. "Good night...."

"Yeah...." Joyce turned and hurried down the flight line toward two pilots waiting near a Huey that was presently being loaded.

Well, hell, Nolan thought as he made his way toward the chow hall tent near Ops, the place where his copilot had been severely poisoned three days ago. He noticed as he approached the huge tent, with its olive-green tarpaulin, that the line was shorter tonight. Navy cooks clothed in white uniforms stood in a row in one corner of the tent, behind large rectangular pans filled with steaming food.

Grabbing an aluminum tray from the teetering stack, Nolan trudged tiredly over to the line. He noticed a number of pilots he knew ahead of him, inching toward the food service. A few strings of naked lightbulbs had been rigged up beneath the tent canopy, illuminating benches and tables below. The buzz of conversation was low but constant. Many of the flight personnel, plus men and women who fueled the birds, crew chiefs and their teams who kept the helos flying and repaired them, were in here, too. Usually, nighttime meant fewer flights, because all available pilots had flown their maximum hours.

Frowning, Nolan wiped his face on his sleeve. He needed a shave. At the small tent where he and his copilot slept, there wasn't a razor or water. A lot of the normal amenities had been blown to the wind with this continuing crisis.

Looking ahead, he spotted a tall woman in an olive-green flight suit waiting her turn in the chow line. It was *her* again—the woman with the gorgeous black hair. Who was she? Nolan frowned. As she stood there confidently, he stared at the patches on her uniform. On the left upper shoulder was the American flag. As she turned, he saw the squadron patch on her shoulder. His squadron. But she was new. A replacement, maybe? Did Joyce know about her? And then he scowled darkly. Damn women. He didn't like them as pilots. Lucky for him, he'd never been assigned with one, and he was glad. He preferred flying with a guy.

Still, as she turned and looked around the chow hall, Nolan found himself watching her with interest. She had an angular profile, with that slightly hawklike nose, those high cheekbones and large, expressive eyes. He allowed his gaze to linger on her like a bee feasting on a flower. The rudimentary lighting in the tent made for a lot of shadows, and leached out everyone's skin color. Though she looked pale beneath the lights, she seemed to have golden skin tones. Most of all, he liked her beautiful, long black hair, which streamed down over her shoulders like a cloak. Nolan's fingers itched to touch that silky mane.

He laughed to himself, figuring he was so damn tired he felt drunk. This wasn't the time or place to be thinking about women! Besides, from the looks of it, she was a pilot. Had she been coming to report for duty when he'd seen her earlier today? He knew all the pilots in his squadron. Maybe she was a replacement? But if she was, she'd have a different squadron patch on her flight uniform. He shook his head. Nothing made sense to him. The earthquake had thrown everyone into chaos, and Nolan tried to pay attention to little, everyday things to keep him sane in this insane emergency. But this woman threw him for a loop.

She was a looker, there was no doubt. Nolan knew that ordinarily one-piece, olive-green flight suits were not sexy looking in the least. They were drab and hung like potato sacks on everyone. But she made hers look good. Lean like a greyhound, she was small breasted though her hips flared just enough for the flight suit to show her womanly attributes. Maybe it was the psychosis of his present sleep deprivation that spiked his desires, but Nolan decided he liked her mouth most of all. It was full and soft looking. Very kissable. Of course, he was too dog tired to even follow that thought. Even if a woman snuggled with him in his sleeping bag at this point, he couldn't do anything about it, he was so exhausted.

Well, at least she was easy on his eyes, a perk he hadn't expected. Moving forward, he watched her go through the line and then sit in a far corner by herself. And then he saw several other pilots looking at her—going over to sit with her after they went through the chow line.

Nolan chuckled himself. He didn't hold it against the guys. They were all single and had an eye for an attractive woman, too. However, he wouldn't even consider sitting with a woman Marine Corps pilot. No way. He preferred his women out of the military—nice, soft civilian types, not hard-edged female officers, who were usually tougher than nails. As he held up his tray to receive his food, Nolan congratulated himself. He wasn't going to go over and introduce himself to this new woman pilot. Let the slavering wolves—the younger guys—do that. Instead, he was going to eat his food, go to his tent and, he hoped, get a good night's sleep. At 0500 tomorrow, he was going to pray that Joyce had found him a copilot, so he could fly to the aid of those desperate families.

January 8: 0545

Nolan scowled as the first light of dawn sent a gray ribbon across the eastern horizon. He was walking down the flight line toward his Huey when he saw another pilot standing by the opened door of the fuselage, inspecting the load of water. Nolan rubbed his sleep-ridden eyes. The shadowy morning light was playing tricks on him, he thought, trying to make out the figure by his Huey. It had to be his new copilot. In Nolan's hand was an order, just signed by Joyce over at Flight Ops, for him to take Lieutenant R. McGregor on as his new copilot. He'd thanked Joyce effusively. She had told him Lieutenant Mc-Gregor was his permanent copilot replacement for the duration of the earthquake relief flights. Further, he'd heard that his old copilot was successfully recovering from the deadly food poisoning in that Seattle hospital. For Nolan, things didn't get any better than this.

His jaw prickled and he rubbed the tender skin where he'd cut himself shaving earlier. Someone had thoughtfully left a bowl of water, some soap and a razor outside his tent. But trying to shave with a mirror and flashlight had proved disastrous. He'd nicked his face at least three different times. As he shaved, he had seen the trucks coming from the C-141s that had flown in last night with supplies. His tent stood in a line with forty others, barely a quarter of a mile from the runway. Usually when a Starlifter came in, the vibrations of the massive engines caused the tents to shake. He'd slept through it all, such was the extent of his exhaustion.

This morning, hope threaded through him as he quickened his pace toward his chopper. He had a new copilot! A permanent one! He saw the guy leaning into the open fuselage, making sure the cargo netting was holding the boxes in place. Good, he liked a copilot who was thorough and efficient and didn't miss such details. Yes, life was looking good to Nolan. His step lightened considerably as he drew up behind his new copilot.

"Lieutenant McGregor?" he demanded.

Rhona gasped. The man's voice was practically in her ear. She straightened and whirled around.

Nolan's mouth fell open. It was the woman in last night's chow line! The very same one he'd seen heading for Logistics with such determination. Today, her black hair was caught up in a French twist, off her shoulders. Her gray eyes were huge and startled looking.

"Who are *you?*" he demanded, taking a step away from her. This couldn't be his copilot! Yet, as Nolan raked his eyes over her upper body, he saw a set of gold aviator's wings stitched onto her flight suit on one side, and the name R. McGregor in gold letters on the black leather name patch above her left breast pocket. No! This couldn't be happening! Not to him! Not a *woman* copilot!

Rhona stared at the six-foot-tall Marine Corps officer. He was looking at her like she was a snake ready to bite him. Gathering her nerves, which were frazzled by his booming voice, Rhona thrust out her hand.

"I'm Rhona McGregor, Lieutenant Galway. I'm your new copilot. Nice to meet you."

Nolan stared at her long, thin hand. Her fingers were slender, graceful, but with blunt-cut nails—no nonsense hands. A flyer's hands. That realization ran through his shocked mind before he could stop it. Even worse, he was discovering she was even more attractive in the dawn light than she had been last night in the chow tent. She wore small, unobtrusive pearl earrings in her delicate ears. Her face was oval, her eyes warm, a slight smile pulling at the corners of her soft mouth. There wasn't anything to dislike about this woman. Not a damn thing, except that she was his copilot!

"I'm Galway, all right," he snarled. "But you can't be R. McGregor. I'm lookin' for a *male* copilot." He hooked his thumb across his shoulder toward Ops. "Lieutenant Mason just assigned me a Lieutenant R. McGregor. That can't be you." And yet, as he stared again at the name plate on her uniform, Nolan finally grasped the fact that it was. His stomach sank. His anger simmered. Joyce hadn't mentioned his copilot's gender. No, she had smiled brightly at him when he'd entered Ops earlier, waved a set of orders at him, telling him the good news. Nolan would have kissed her, if military rules allowed it. He'd been so thrilled at her finding him a partner, that he hadn't asked any questions. Apparently, he should have.

Rhona was taken aback. She saw the dark cloud of anger on Lieutenant Galway's rugged, square face. Nolan Galway wasn't pretty-boy handsome, but he had a strength in his face she instantly liked. And she couldn't resist the boyish freckles sprinkled across his nose and cheeks. Maybe it was the stubborn set of his jaw, or his large, intelligent eyes. Or his mouth, which was now thinned in obvious disapproval.

"Excuse me?" She dropped her hand. The fact that he wasn't going to shake it put her on warning that he didn't like *her*. "I'm Rhona McGregor," she repeated.

"Lieutenant Mason assigned me to you this morning as your replacement copilot for the duration of the disaster relief effort." She frowned, tensing inwardly to protect herself from his anger. Her stomach automatically clenched.

Nolan, who normally had glib words for every occasion, stood there speechless. Rhona was tall, lean—beautiful. And God help him, he liked her gray eyes, so bright with intelligence. But as her arched black brows drew downward, he steeled himself.

"They didn't say you were a woman," he sputtered angrily.

"Gender has no place in this, Lieutenant Galway," she stated, then clenched her teeth. Great! He was a Neanderthal! Rhona's heart sank. Not another one! She'd left the navy precisely because of men like the one standing in front of her. This guy wasn't going to respect her as an aviator who could do just as good of a job at the stick as he could.

"Look," Nolan growled, "this isn't going to work out. I fly with men only. Okay?" Yet his mind was racing. Copilots didn't grow on trees. Joyce had said McGregor was the only one available, that replacements weren't going to be coming in for another three days, the flights into Camp Reed were so stacked up.

Rhona felt a spurt of anger. "Beggars can't be choosers, Lieutenant Galway." Her eyes narrowed. "And from where I'm standing, if I were in your shoes, I'd be grateful for whoever showed up to help you pilot this bird."

Rubbing his mouth, he took another step away from

her. "Look, I just don't like women in the cockpit with me, okay?"

"You'll have to put up with it, Lieutenant. This isn't up to you."

"Just who the hell are you, anyway? You're wearin' our squadron patch and you're not one of us."

Rhona sat down on the lip of the Huey, her hands clasped between her thighs. Galway had gall. A lot of it. She eyed him assessingly before speaking. "I used to fly in the navy, Lieutenant. I've been out six months. I'm still air qualified on Hueys and CH-46E Sea Knights. I volunteered my services here at Ops yesterday. They were glad to see me. Too bad you aren't. I'm here to help those people out there." She pointed in the direction of the L.A. basin. "What are you here to do? The same thing, I hope."

Stung, he glared at her. All up and down the flight line, things were starting to get busy. Pilots were coming out to check their birds before they took off for the first of many flights today. Cargo masters with lists in hand were double-checking the loads aboard the Hueys.

"This is a mistake. A *big* one. Joyce knows I don't fly with women. And besides, you're a civilian! That's not allowed. You can't just resign your navy commission and step in here and start flying again."

Rhona saw the desperation in his taut face, the downward curve of his mouth. Oh, he had a wonderful-looking mouth, in her opinion, and under any other circumstances, Nolan Galway would be the kind of tall, dark and handsome man she would go for. But not now. His looks didn't do a damn thing for her at the moment.

"Luckily, that isn't for you to decide. Ops was fine with my credentials. You will be, too." She left off the "or else" because Rhona had no desire to fan the conflagration occurring between them right now.

Nolan paced. On the one hand, if he went back to complain to Joyce, she might remove him from the roster due to gender harassment. This wasn't acceptable behavior, Nolan knew. No, if he complained to Ops, more than likely he'd get his tail in a bind and wouldn't be allowed to fly at all. *Damn.*

"Look at the real reason I'm here," Rhona told him grimly. "I walked in from Bonsall yesterday. I saw the devastation. I know you're running shorthanded because all the pilots have eaten up their mandatory flight time under FAA laws. I volunteered, Lieutenant Galway, because I *care* for the people out there." Again she jabbed her finger toward the west. "And I *can* make a difference. Now, if you have an objection to me being a woman, that's *your* problem. Not the Marine Corps's. Not mine. I think you'd better widen your vision. Let go of that narrow-mindedness and look at the bigger picture. Why are you taking these missions? Just to fly? Or are you trying to help people who are starving to death out there? Who are thirsty? Or who might need medical help?"

Rhona stood up, placed her hands on her hips and held his stormy green gaze. "That's why I'm here. Why the hell are you standing there? To get more flight hours?" That was an insult and Rhona knew it.

Anger sizzled through Nolan. Especially when he saw that they'd given her the rank of first lieutenant— the same as his. She was his equal in every way under military law. In fact, her rank made her a full-fledged pilot, so she wasn't really his copilot. That meant her skills were commensurate to his, whether he liked to admit it or not.

Running his fingers distractedly through his hair, he glared at her. "Climb down off your high horse, will you, McGregor? Okay, you're my co. I don't like it, but I'm not gonna argue any further under the circumstances." He saw his crew chief, Corporal Tavis Burt, ambling toward them. "It's time to turn and burn, McGregor. You say you know Hueys. Well, I'll be watching your every move until I'm satisfied you know what the hell you're doing in that cockpit with me. If you've been out six months, your skills are gonna be rusty. You just sit in that seat and I'll do the flying. As far as I'm concerned, you're just a pretty bauble taking up space in my cockpit to fulfill military and FAA requirements, and that's it. I don't need you. I don't need your help or your input. Got it?"

A wave of hurt washed through Rhona. She stood there, digging her fingers into her hips to stop the anger from spilling out. The venom in his look, in his words, scalded her. She saw the crew chief, a young man with red hair and blue eyes, hurrying toward them.

"Yeah, I hear you, Lieutenant Galway," she said with gritted teeth.

With a sharp nod of his head, he snarled, "Fine.

Now make your walk-around, Lieutenant, and I'll talk to my crew chief.''

The bastard. Rhona allowed her tense hands to drop from her hips. The walk-around was a necessary component of flying. She had to look for hydraulic leaks, make sure that all surfaces were intact and that nothing was loose or leaking. Beginning at the nose, she slowly moved around the Huey, her hand skimming the fuselage almost lovingly as she checked out the bird.

Trying to put Nolan Galway and his acidic hatred of her out of her mind, Rhona kept one ear tuned to the conversation between him and the soft-spoken, gangly crew chief, who looked to be in his midtwenties. Rarely did an aircraft have all instruments operational. There was always something that was down or needed to be fixed, but wasn't essential to the act of flying. A crew chief went over those errors with the pilot, so he knew ahead of time that a button, knob or piece of software wasn't working right. If it was bad enough, the bird would be grounded until the spare part could be replaced. As Rhona looked up to check the tail rotor of the Huey, she saw that the young crew chief had dark circles under his eyes. The realization that everyone was working long, arduous hours with little sleep hit her again.

As she came around to the fuselage door, where the dark green nylon netting held the cargo in place, the crew chief looked up. When he approached her, saluted and came to attention, Rhona did the same.

"At ease, Chief," she murmured. "I'm Lieutenant McGregor. Nice to meet you."

He flushed. "Yes, ma'am, same here."

Rhona saw Galway enter the chopper through the door and work his way forward to the right seat, where the pilot sat. She focused her attention on the nervous crew chief. He had acne, which had scarred most of his face, leaving it pockmarked. Feeling for him, she smiled slightly.

"What do I need to know about this Huey, Chief? What's down with it?"

"Well, ma'am," the corporal said unhappily, "the navigation software is out. Totally."

Frowning, Rhona said, "That's reason enough to ground this bird, Chief. Why haven't you?"

"Well…er, ma'am, Lieutenant Galway is the pilot and he has final say on whether or not it's a go. He says he can do visuals and get to area six with no problem."

Glancing up at the dawn sky, Rhona saw that it was cloudy, and looked like rain. Rhona said nothing. The chief was right: the pilot would make the final determination on this. "Okay. So, I get to play navigator today. Is that it?"

Flushing slightly, he gave her a soft smile. "Yes, ma'am, I'm afraid so. Do you have any problems with that? Lieutenant Galway says you've been out of the navy for six months."

Holding on to her simmering anger, Rhona said, "Not a problem, Chief." She took the clipboard and pen he was holding toward her and signed off on the flight status of the helicopter and the fact that navigation software was inoperable. "What's the prognosis on getting this fixed, Chief?"

Grimacing, he reclaimed the clipboard. "Not good, ma'am. I had my team look at it last night, about 0100, and it's fried."

"That means you need to have new software installed?"

"Yes, ma'am, it does." Hitching his thin shoulders, he gave her a sad look. "Unfortunately, Ops has relegated such things to the back burner because of the need for live-and-die supplies comin' into Camp Reed first."

"I see," Rhona murmured sympathetically. She gave him a perfunctory smile. "Well, no problem. I'm sure Mr. Galway can fly his route with his eyes closed. Thanks for your help. We'll see you on the return trip."

Coming to attention and saluting, the chief said, "Yes, ma'am! Thank you…." He backed off and went to untether the blades and remove the chocks from beneath the wheels.

Climbing into the chopper, Rhona moved forward, squeezing past the cargo and between the two seats. The chief slid the door closed and locked it behind her. Nolan was busy, she saw, and sat down. The familiarity of harnessing up, getting her copilot checklist situated on her knee board, felt good. Around them, the world was waking up. More trucks arrived, their bellicose diesel voices echoing up and down the flight line. Up ahead, the first Huey of the ten in line took off, heading for the area it was to service. They were number six in line for takeoff.

"Let's get to it," Nolan growled, indicating their checklist.

"Fine." Rhona sat ready, pencil in hand to tick off each item.

Nolan purposely ran through the preflight list fast. If he thought she was going to be slow or stupid, he was wrong. Her hand flew knowingly over each knob, each switch on the instrument panel. She was graceful, each movement flowing into the next. Only a pilot who had flown the Huey for a long time had that kind of familiarity with the location of each item in the cockpit. Well, maybe McGregor wasn't as inept as he'd feared, after all, but he wasn't about to hand the chopper over to her. No, as far as Nolan was concerned, she was nothing more than a hood ornament in that left seat, there only because of military and FAA flight regulations.

"Where's your flak vest?" he demanded, setting his notebook in a net pocket behind his seat.

Frowning, Rhona realized he had on a flak vest, plus a .45 pistol in a black leather holster strapped across his chest.

"They didn't issue me one."

"Great." He sat there stewing. Should he make her go get a vest and pistol, or just take off? Shaking his head, he muttered, "When we get back, get your butt over to Supply and get a vest and pistol."

"Fine, I will."

"It's dangerous out there, McGregor. You look like

Miss Innocence and I know the world's probably a fluffy pink bubble to you, but out there—'' he jabbed his index finger toward the Plexiglas cockpit window ''—is trouble with a capital *T*. The area I fly into is a Latino barrio. The people there are nice enough, but with a lack of supplies, I'm not sure how long it will be before gang warfare breaks out. If we run into any trouble on this flight mission, you're going to wish you had that vest and pistol.'' He turned and looked at her. ''You can go get it now. I'll make the flight and come back and pick you up.''

He was trying to intimidate her. ''I'm touched by your concern, Lieutenant, but I think you got this backward. You *can't* fly without me in this seat and you know it.''

Shrugging, he muttered, ''No one will know. Just you and me.''

Rhona glared at him. ''And you don't think I'll tell Ops, is that it? Are you setting me up to be the fall person here, Lieutenant? You know that if I do report that you're flying this bird alone, they'll can your butt. But that will also make me out to be a stool pigeon. How convenient.''

Nolan saw the anger and hurt in her huge gray eyes. His conscience ate at him. McGregor was probably a nice enough woman. But he simply didn't want her in his cockpit. ''Yeah...okay...so sit there. But when we land, you stay in this bird. You do *not* get out of it. That's an order. You hear me?''

''I hear you, Lieutenant. Loud and clear.''

Three

Nolan tried to ignore Rhona's whiskey-soft voice as she called in to the tower for clearance to take off. The Huey was shaking and shuddering around them, and the vibration felt comforting to him. Right now, he was tense with her in his cockpit. Yet, grudgingly, he acknowledged so far she'd done everything she was supposed to flawlessly, and with the touch of a professional.

Glancing at her out the corner of his eye, he saw the sharpness of her profile. She almost looked Indian to him, with that slightly curved, thin nose. Her skin was indeed golden-toned. And she had high cheekbones and black hair. But her eyes were gray. Maybe a half-breed? Nolan mentally corrected himself. He shouldn't be thinking like that. It was a derogatory term, and it could get him in a lot of trouble with his superiors if he ever said it aloud. The last thing he needed was to be hauled up on racial or sexual harassment charges. Flying with a woman was going to force him to watch what he said, because he was used to working with men who shared a common understanding.

"Ready for takeoff?" Rhona asked him. She repositioned the microphone near her lips. The helmet she wore was one from the pilot ready room, and didn't fit her as well as she'd like, but now was not the time to ask to have a helmet made for her. Most pilots had helmets shaped and fitted to their skull, making them comfortable to wear for long hours.

Rhona drew down the dark shield that covered the upper half of her face as the sun peeked above the horizon before them. She noted Galway did the same.

"Roger. Ready for takeoff." He notched up the engine power on the Huey.

The familiar swift shuddering as the chopper's blades whirled faster and faster was thrilling to Rhona. She sat with her gloved hands on her thighs. Doubting that Nolan was going to trust her to do anything in the cockpit, she relaxed and decided to memorize their flight route.

The Huey lifted off and nosed down slightly as Galway coaxed the dark green helicopter up and forward. Ahead of them, Rhona could see the five other Hueys that had already lifted off. After they cleared Camp

Reed airport airspace, they looked like a long line of geese in flight. Then, one by one, each banked and flew off to their assigned area within the quake zone.

"Each helo has a specific area assigned to it?" Rhona asked.

Nolan nodded. "Yeah. I have area six. It's a two-square-mile piece of southern L.A. real estate in a Latino barrio."

She noticed he said "I" and not "we." Rhona didn't like the fact that he was trying to freeze her out. Stung once again, but saying nothing about it, she offered, "You want me to figure out the navigation for you?"

"No. I can fly this route blindfolded." His heart sped up. Rhona McGregor was saying and doing all the right things a co would do for a pilot. He saw her full lips tighten. She was gazing around as he leveled off at three thousand feet.

"Looks like rain coming." Rhona lifted her gloved hand and pointed in the direction they were flying. Below them, the undulating sandy, sage-brush-covered hills of Camp Reed were a blur. Ahead, Rhona could see the first signs of civilization, where the military reservation ended and the crowded suburbs of Los Angeles began. The houses made her think of rats in a maze: too many people in too small an area.

"What did meteorology say?" Nolan demanded, frowning at the dark gray scud that obliterated part of the western horizon. Had Rhona gotten the weather report? A good co would have.

"Weather desk said eighty percent chance of rain

by 1400. Right now, we've got a cold front coming through. It's a fast one, with a pretty hefty lowering of the barometric pressure.''

"Yeah," Nolan grumbled, "I can feel the wind tugging at her.''

Smiling to herself, Rhona noticed he referred to the Huey he flew as a "her." That wasn't uncommon. Most men considered the aircraft they flew as feminine. She didn't. To her, it was a "he." The different gender dynamics were interesting, she mused.

"It's 0625 now," Nolan said. "If I get help from the people in the barrio, which I usually do when I land, they'll off-load this bottled water and we can do a quick turnaround.''

"This cargo is going to supply enough water for a two-square-mile area filled with people?" Rhona glanced back at the cargo anchored solidly beneath the olive-drab nylon netting.

Snorting, Nolan said, "Hell no! We can't even begin to get enough water in to them. There's a ground crew going in there today, a sergeant and a squad of marines. They're going to set up an H.Q. in the barrio, try to figure out numbers of people, their needs and medical status. At the moment, however, I'm the only link they've got to the outside world.''

Groaning, Rhona murmured, "That must be awful for them.''

He glanced at her. "It's not a pretty sight. People are hungry. They're scared. They feel naked and vulnerable out there. There's civil unrest, but with no police department to speak of, the place is in chaos. That's why we wear flak vests and carry a weapon.'' She was looking at him with soulful and compassionate eyes. Beautiful eyes, Nolan decided. The kind a man could drown in. Although her features were sharply defined, he found her arrestingly attractive. A strand of black hair had escaped near her temple and was peeking out from beneath the helmet she wore. The maddening urge to lift his hand and tuck that lock back into place with his finger surprised the hell out of Nolan. He didn't want her in his cockpit. He didn't want a female copilot at all. Yet, from a masculine standpoint, he was reacting powerfully to her quiet, unassuming presence.

Scowling, he decided it was because she was a woman. Just being around one, Nolan found himself wanting to open up and talk. He had to continually stop himself from indulging in the normal chatter he had in the cockpit. Usually, he had some jokes to share, stories and small talk. But not today. And certainly not with her. Maybe if he could make her uncomfortable enough, not allow her to do anything except sit there, she'd get the hint and ask for a transfer to another pilot's Huey.

Of course, he might not get a replacement for her, Nolan calculated. Joyce had said that it would be no less than three days before a slate of fresh helicopter pilots could be flown in to help in relief efforts. Until then, Nolan might be stuck with her. *Damn.* Too bad she was so cocksure. There wasn't a shred of hesitancy in Rhona McGregor. She obviously knew what she was doing.

"So, is there gunplay where we're going?" Rhona now wished she'd gotten a flak vest and pistol. On their return trip, she'd hitch a ride over to Supply and pick them up. For sure.

"So far, no," Nolan said. He banked the Huey as they flew over hills covered with homes. The wind was gusty, which was typical when a front was coming through. The gray, scudding clouds in the west were moving swiftly toward them. Behind them, the sun had risen and was peeking shyly from between the long filaments of clouds. It was a depressing-looking day compared to the normally sunny California weather.

Rhona realized she was going to have to ask a lot of questions to get answers about their flight route and landing area. Nolan wasn't going to volunteer anything. If she were a man, he'd probably be a chatterbox. Anger flared again. Yet when he spoke, she heard the concern in his voice for the people they were flying to help. She also saw it in the way the corners of his full mouth quirked. He might be a male chauvinist pig, a Neanderthal, but he *did* care. That was a point on the good side of Nolan Galway, as far as Rhona was concerned. She noticed how his hands wrapped around the cyclic and collective, the gentle touch he had with them. He wasn't one of those pilots that jerked a helicopter around, was rough or heavy-handed. No, he was smooth as a good sip of fruit brandy sliding down her throat after a long, hot day in the cockpit of her crop-dusting chopper. Rhona didn't want to like him, because of his demeanor toward her, but she did admire his desire to help people in need. Maybe he wasn't the villain she'd first thought. Maybe, with time, he'd settle down and accept her as a partner, a member of his team.

Below, the expensive, red-tile-roofed homes began to disappear, replaced by stucco houses in bright pastel colors, with brown roofing. All of them had been flattened and dismantled by the quake.

"See that dried-up square of yellow grass at two o'clock?" he said.

Squinting, Rhona saw the rectangular area—a kind of plaza with houses squeezed around it. "Yes."

"That's the barrio's softball field. Doesn't look like much because there's been little rain this year, but that's where we land. Señor Manuel Gonzalez is the senior man in the barrio. He's responsible for getting the people to work together as a team. Nice old gentleman. Probably in his eighties. He's got pure white hair and wears thick glasses. The ol' gent can barely see, but he's got a heart as big as this basin. And he's a natural leader. The people love him, respect him." Nolan smiled briefly as he eased the Huey down to a thousand feet, approaching the baseball diamond. "I'm lucky he's there. He's set a schedule of who gets what, and when. Everyone lets him do this. They realize he's fair, and everyone gets something." Mouth quirking, Nolan muttered, "And it isn't much. The people have pretty much gone through all their canned foodstuffs and are now going hungry."

"But they're willing to trust Señor Gonzalez to dole out what we bring in to the barrio? Without a fight?"

"Yes, so far…" Nolan saw a small knot of people standing near the four long rows of wooden bleachers that were scattered due to the quake, waiting patiently for the chopper.

"Why do you say so far?" Rhona demanded. She looked around. There was a group of about ten men standing at the edge of the ball field, watching them. Nolan brought the Huey to a hover and then began to descend for the landing. As the bird came down, the dust from the playing field began to rise around it, until thick yellow clouds rose skyward. There was a gentle jolt and they were on the ground. Nolan cut the power.

"Don't you want to keep the engine on idle?"

He shook his head. "No. It's a way of conserving fuel. Orders from Ops. This is our new SOP—standard operating procedure." Nolan unplugged the jack from his helmet and then took the helmet off. He jabbed a finger at her.

"You stay *here.*"

Nodding, Rhona said nothing. She watched as Nolan set down his helmet and then squeezed between the seats. He opened the rear door, sliding it wide and locking it so it couldn't shut accidentally. The blades were slowing down and the dust was settling. She saw a white-haired man, probably Señor Gonzalez, coming forward with a decided limp. He leaned heavily on a carved wooden cane. The men with him, all young and in their twenties, followed him respectfully. They didn't surge ahead. They didn't charge at the helicopter.

Rhona twisted around in her seat and watched as Nolan quickly unhooked the nylon webbing around the boxes and threw it off to one side. As the blades slowed to a halt, the group approached the helicopter. Nolan grinned at them, a smile that lit up his entire face. He reached out of the helicopter, his hand extended to the white-haired gentleman. Rhona saw genuine delight and care in Nolan's face as he gently gripped the Mexican leader's old, arthritic hand. The smile on Manuel Gonzalez's face was just as heartfelt.

Quickly, the group of young men started taking the cardboard boxes filled with bottled water out of the rear of the Huey. Looking at the stacked boxes, Rhona realized with a sinking feeling that there wasn't nearly enough water to supply so many people for half a day. What were they finding to drink? There were no wells around here. The earthquake had destroyed the pipes that carried the city's water. Her heart bled as she watched Nolan ease out of the chopper and stand beside Manuel. The young men backed up an old flatbed truck, placing each box upon it for later distribution.

Nolan patted the old man's shoulder and then, giving him a salute, turned and climbed back into the helicopter. He slid the door shut and moved forward into the cockpit.

"Want me to take the flight back?" Rhona asked him once he'd plugged in the phone jack and resettled his helmet on his head.

"No. I'll fly." His tone was dark. He didn't want

her doing anything. She could damn well sit there and watch. His hand flew knowingly across the instrument panel, and he saw her nod. Her face relayed no displeasure, but her eyes—those soft, velvety eyes of hers—narrowed slightly. Then she pulled out the preflight card on her thigh board. Good, she was going to be a copilot and do what was necessary, on time.

Within ten minutes, they had lifted off and were heading back toward Camp Reed. Rhona looked around the barrio as they gained altitude above it. She saw a few people moving about, though it was still early morning. In the distance, about a mile from the baseball field, she noted a thick, black column of smoke.

"What's that? A house fire?"

Nolan glanced where she was pointing. "Yeah. When fires start now, there's no way to put them out. No water." He turned and looked at her. She had her face shield up, so he could see her expression. Again he was struck by her possible Indian heritage.

"What a shame," she murmured. "I'm just beginning to realize the full extent of this emergency." Shaking her head, she said, "When I walked from Bonsall to Camp Reed, I was heading out of the suburbs, so I didn't see all of this...." She opened her hand and gestured gracefully. "All this destruction..."

"I know what you mean." He brought the Huey back up to three thousand feet and aimed its nose toward Camp Reed. Again the familiar shaking and shuddering was soothing to Nolan. His gaze flicked rapidly and continually across the instrument panel. A part of him liked conversing with Rhona. She was obviously deeply touched by the plight of the people. He'd seen it written all over her face when he'd come back into the cockpit. There'd been tears in her eyes. Or maybe his imagination was playing tricks on him. But when he looked up at her again, her mouth was pursed with pain. From what little he knew about her, Nolan figured it was her emotional reaction to the plight of the people they were trying to help.

"When me and my co started this flight route to area six, we didn't have a *clue* as to what it all meant." Grimly, Nolan glanced over at her. "I do now. We're eight days into this crisis. FEMA, the Federal Emergency Management Agency, is working out of Camp Reed, and telling us to expect it to get a lot worse. When we get that squad of marines into the barrio today, we'll start getting numbers on the people there, and that will help Logistics know how many choppers to send in and with what kind of food, medicine and water supplies they need long-term. The squad will act as census takers of a sort, relaying the info to Logistics, so they can plan for the future."

Shaking her head, Rhona whispered, "Nolan, it won't be enough. Camp Reed's airport is small. It's overwhelmed with air traffic now. And we don't have near the number of helicopters we need to service these areas."

"Tell me about it," he mumbled unhappily. Though he was trying desperately not to let the fact that she'd called him by his first name affect him, his skin prickled pleasantly. He focused on his flying. Above all else, he couldn't let Rhona get to him. He had to keep her at arm's length.

As Rhona sat there, the enormity of the disaster sank in. "My God, that means…" She turned to him, her eyes huge. "That means that no matter how many people are in that barrio, or any other area, we're not going to be able to supply enough food or water for them to survive this. Are we?"

The tremble in her voice caught him off guard. But the tears welling up in her gray eyes were his undoing. "Don't go soft on me, McGregor, dammit." His voice was hoarse. "I don't need a crybaby in the cockpit with me. So buck up. We'll save who we can. We'll do the best we can. And no, we aren't gonna be able to save the world, so get used to it."

His voice was rough and his words were harsh. Jerking his gaze from her softening face, Nolan forced himself to pay attention to his job. He saw that the undulating golden hills peppered with cactus and sagebrush were already racing by beneath them.

Sitting there, the shock rolling through her, Rhona could say little. Taking a deep breath, she curled her hands into fists. She didn't want to believe Nolan, but she knew in her heart that he was right. One helicopter could carry only so much cargo on each trip.

Swallowing hard, she rasped, "How many trips do you make a day?"

Nolan laughed. The sound was hoarse, hopeless. "Not enough, that's for damned sure."

"How many?"

He heard the steely note in her voice.

"Ten on a good day."

"And that's with you flying all the time?"

"Yes."

"And then you stop?"

"Yes."

"Nolan, it can't escape you that if you'd let your copilot take over, we could fly *more* trips. FAA regs allow a pilot to fly only so many flight hours in a twenty-four-hour period. We could double it if you'd let me fly."

Glancing at her, he heard the hope, the desperation, in her voice. "We have to sleep, too, you know. I've been at this eight days now, and we've been burning the candle at both ends. Between me and my copilot, we were flying twelve hours nonstop. But that's flight time, not ground time, or loading or unloading or fueling time, McGregor. Put it all together, and we were in this cockpit for eighteen hours a day. You can do that for only so long and then you get tired. Bone tired. And you gotta take a rest whether you want to or not. That's how it is."

Rattled emotionally by the people's plight, Rhona saw his rationale. "So what are we doing today?" She purposely used the word *we*. She also noted that Nolan's voice had been tinged with longing when he spoke of his previous partner. She knew she couldn't replace the other co, but she could fly.

As he saw her pick up the mike to call the control tower for permission to land at the upcoming airport, Nolan grimaced. After she received permission and hung up the mike on the console, he felt her eyes on him. His conscience burning him, he sensed what she was about to ask.

"Are you going to let me fly today?"

"I'm not sure...."

"Why not?" Anger stirred in Rhona. She saw him begin to drop altitude as they made the dogleg turn into the landing pattern. From the air, too, Camp Reed looked like a virtual beehive of activity.

"Just because!" Nolan snarled. He didn't want this conversation. He knew he was being stubborn when he shouldn't be, but dammit, he couldn't help himself.

"You don't want me to fly because I'm a woman, and you prefer a man sitting here," she said in a low, quavering tone. Glaring at him, she saw his mouth set, as if he wanted to refute her words. The Huey banked as he brought it in for a landing, the ground blurring beneath them. "And you're willing to sacrifice people's lives because you're so damned shortsighted and prejudiced. If you would let me fly my six hours, we could double the amount of supplies we take to area six. But you aren't going to do that, are you, Lieutenant? Why? Because you're pigheaded, that's why. Oh, I have this little game of yours figured out. And I'll be damned if I'll let you get away with it. Your priorities are all screwed up. Well, mine aren't." She jabbed her finger downward. "The minute we land, I'm going to Ops and I'm talking to the major. You're going to let me fly or else. I care too much for the people we're trying to help to let your prejudice stop me from flying this bird."

Four

January 8: 0700

Rhona was breathing hard, and she tried to control her spiraling anger as they disembarked from the Huey. Immediately, a truck crew hurried forward to begin putting box after box of bottled water into the cargo hold of the bird. Simultaneously, a fueling crew brought the huge green tanker over, and a woman pulled the nozzle toward their chopper to fill it up for another flight.

Rhona walked determinedly at Galway's shoulder. His face was dark, his eyes flashing with anger, his mouth thin and set. Since they both had enough sense to talk out of earshot of enlisted people, Nolan led her off to one side of the black asphalt apron, then rounded on her.

Instantly, Rhona put her hands belligerently on her hips. Nostrils flaring, her eyes slitted, she waited for the expected hailstorm of venom to spew from him. In her heart, she didn't want this confrontation. She liked Nolan, despite his obvious prejudice toward her. He had his own heart in the right place; she'd seen the genuine concern in his eyes and voice as he'd talked to Señor Gonzalez.

"Look," Nolan snarled, "I don't like this one bit."

"What? Me being a woman pilot?"

Glaring, he held her steadily in his narrowed green gaze. There was nothing weak or passive about Rhona. She was a warrior through and through, and he recognized that. But damn, why did she have to be so alluring to him? What was it about her exotic face? Those soft lips, now pursed? And those heartbreaking gray eyes, which could go rabbit soft with compassion and touch him so effortlessly and deeply?

Nolan stood there, tense and stiff. He leaned forward, deliberately trying to intimidate her, for he was three inches taller than she was. "I *prefer* a man in the cockpit with me."

"Tough, Lieutenant. You don't get everything you want in the military. We both know that." Rhona's voice quavered. "You're going to stand here and tell me that, as pilot in command, you're going to limit us to six hours of flight time because *I'm* in the cockpit with you? When we could double that time and get that many more supplies to all the starving, thirsty people? I can't believe your conscience, the humanity I saw in you back there, would allow you to make that decision.'' She flung the last words back at him like a gauntlet. Rhona knew how to face off with Neanderthals. She saw the surprise in his eyes, the flare of realization as her fiery words hit their mark and exposed the truth of the situation. Mentally, she was urging him to make the right decision. Her intuition told her that as much of a caveman as Galway was, he wouldn't forsake people in need just because of his own prejudice. At least she hoped he wouldn't.

Coming out of his confrontational posture, Nolan took a step back. Angrily he shoved his fingers through his dark hair, which was plastered down with sweat from wearing the helmet earlier.

"You don't make things easy, McGregor," he rasped.

"I didn't create this situation, Lieutenant. I came here and *volunteered* my services. I didn't have to do that. I don't have to stand here and take this kind of crap from you, either. Now, you either back down, accept me as your copilot and let me fly my six hours in the Huey, or I'm going through the chain of command to get your butt put in a sling so high you'll never see the ground again.'' Her jaw set. "Am I coming through loud and clear to you, Galway?'' She purposely used his last name without the respect of his rank to show him she meant business. And she saw her words landing like rockets being fired. His face went pale. And then a red flush scoured his cheeks.

Nolan stood there, clenching his teeth. She was right

and he knew it. Anger and frustration warred in him as, hands propped defiantly on her hips, her chin jutting out, she confronted him, ready to fight him every step of the way, if necessary. No, he didn't want his career going down the tubes over this. It wasn't worth it. Rubbing his chin, he stood there studying Rhona. Damn, she was beautiful. Too bad she was an ex-military pilot. And his copilot. Otherwise he could think of more pleasurable ways of spending time with her.

"Okay," he growled, "you win this round, McGregor. I'll let you fly every other trip. We'll put in our twelve hours."

Relief washed though Rhona, though she saw he didn't like his decision. Lifting her hands from her hips, she opened them in supplication. "Lieutenant, in my heart, I knew you'd choose the people's needs over your own prejudice. For that, I thank you. You don't have to like me. You don't have to speak to me, other than for operational reasons in the cockpit. I can handle your hatred. I handled it for seven years in the navy, with pilots just like you who didn't want me around." Moving her shoulders to release the tension there, Rhona added, "It's too bad you won't judge me on my abilities, Lieutenant. If you did, you'd find I'm damn good at what I do."

Nolan looked away, focusing on the Huey on the tarmac. He saw that the ground crew already had the bird gassed, loaded and ready to go. He tried to get hold of his escaping emotions because a part of him didn't want to hurt Rhona, and he knew by the look in her eyes that he had. "Get your butt over to Supply," he rasped. "You need to get a flak vest and a pistol. Our bird's ready to go." He pointed to a HumVee nearby. "Hop onboard and tell the driver where you need to go. He'll get you over there and back. Hurry up. We've got people to help."

January 8: 0730

It felt good to be flying again, Rhona admitted to herself as she coaxed the Huey to three thousand feet and leveled off. Having a dual set of controls, the Huey could be flown from either position, and Nolan sat on her right, his profile grim. Since she'd returned to the apron with her new flak vest, which chafed against her skin, and a pistol strapped to the left side of her chest, Nolan hadn't said more than three words to her. Hurt, but trying not to take it personally, Rhona was grateful that his better side had won out. Still, the cockpit was filled with tension. She wished mightily to defuse it, but saw no easy way to do that.

It was 0730, and the sky was lightening up, although the day was gray and the clouds in the west looked more threatening all the time. Still, the Huey felt good in her hands. Sensing Nolan's tightly held emotions, none of which were particularly positive, she stuck to what she did best: flying.

Nolan grudgingly slanted a glance toward Rhona. Her face was soft now, her lips slightly parted as she flew his bird. He didn't want to admit it, but she had a damn light touch with the Huey—a good one. She

was smooth. Smooth as fine silk, and if he didn't have
so much thickheaded pride, he'd admit she was a better pilot than he was. The bird flew flawlessly in her
long-fingered hands. Mouth moving downward, Nolan
scowled and looked out the Plexiglas windshield.
Their area was coming up shortly. To the right, he saw
the black, thick column of smoke rising a good thousand feet into the sky.

"Looks like a whole city block is gonna be up in
flames soon," he said, pointing toward the malevolent-
looking column.

Glancing to where he gestured, Rhona said, "No
water, so the fire's jumping from house to house?"

"Yeah, unfortunately." Shrugging, he added,
"Probably doesn't matter. All the homes are destroyed, anyway. Most of them were flattened by that
mother of a quake."

"People still have their photos, the things that mean
something to them, in that rubble, even if the homes
themselves are destroyed."

Hearing the pain in Rhona's voice, he glanced over
at her. She was looking toward the spreading fire, her
eyes narrowed, her black brows drawn down in concern. Nolan's heart expanded.

The feeling surprised him. Rubbing his chest unconsciously, he wondered what it was about her that
was making him feel like that. And then, when she
swung her gaze momentarily to his, he jerked his head
away and looked in the other direction. She seemed to
have the ability to peer into his soul, and he felt vul-

nerable around her. That scared him. A lot. No woman except one—his wife—had ever had that ability.

"Yeah, you're right. Photos are everything." Didn't he know that? Of course he did. Rhona seemed to have a sensitivity he lacked. But then, that's what separated men from women, he told himself stoically as she started to bring the Huey in for a landing on the baseball diamond. A thousand feet below, he could see Señor Gonzalez with his young men beside the battered flatbed truck, waiting patiently for the next shipment to arrive.

This time, Nolan ordered Rhona out of the cockpit once they powered down and the engine was shut off. He made his way out of the sliding door and onto the ground. Señor Gonzalez moved forward slowly, leaning heavily on the cane in his right hand. The ten Hispanics with him, all tall, athletic young men, stayed behind him respectfully, even though he walked at a snail's pace. As Nolan stood beside the Huey, waiting for Rhona to disembark, he wished that the rest of America's youths would respect their elders as these Latinos did. The country would be a far better place for everyone.

Rhona jumped to the ground beside Nolan and tugged at the chafing flak vest. Her hair was still tightly wrapped so that it stayed in place when she took off her helmet. As she did so she saw Señor Gonzalez's weatherbeaten face light up with surprise and then pleasure.

"Ah, we have a *señorita* pilot, eh, Lieutenant Galway?'' he said by way of greeting as he stopped beside the Huey next to Nolan.

Scowling, Nolan said, ''Yes, sir, we do. This is Lieutenant McGregor. Lieutenant, this is Señor Gonzalez, the leader for area six.''

Rhona stepped aside to allow the young men to start taking boxes out of the Huey and putting them on the truck, which was being slowly backed into place nearby.

''Nice to meet you, sir. I'll be seeing a lot of you in the coming weeks.''

Gripping her gloved hand warmly, the old man lifted it and placed a circumspect kiss on the back. ''We welcome you with open arms and open hearts, Señorita McGregor. Surely you have a first name?'' He smiled and released her hand.

Heat rushed to Rhona's face at the old gentleman's courtly behavior. She'd never had her hand kissed by anyone. ''Why, er, yes, sir, I do. You can call me Rhona.''

Eyes twinkling, Manuel looked at Nolan. ''Not only is she helping you to fly to us, but she is very beautiful. I envy you, Lieutenant Galway.''

Grumpily, Nolan said, ''She's just another pilot, Señor Gonzalez. Nothing more.'' He really didn't mean that, but he couldn't help being testy right now. Seeing the shadow cross Rhona's face at his words, he felt like a heel. Why was he gigging her like this? Because she was a woman in his cockpit, that's why. And Nolan knew that was not a good enough reason. He'd never treat a male copilot like this; he'd never been snotty and snide about anyone in front of others.

Rhona, however, ignored his immature behavior. "*Señor,* are those homes on fire a part of your area?"

"Eh?" Manuel slowly turned and looked at the rising plume of black smoke smudging the sky. "That? No, Señorita Rhona. That is area five."

"How'd the fire start?" Nolan asked, relieved to change the topic.

Shaking his head, Manuel muttered, "They call themselves Diablo, devils, Lieutenant Galway."

"Devils?" Nolan demanded. "Who or what is that?"

"We are receiving word from the people of area five that there is a gang who call themselves Diablo. They are deliberately setting fire to the homes."

"What?" Rhona exclaimed in surprise. "Why on earth would they do that? Isn't there enough havoc and grief without deliberately setting fires?"

"*Sí, señorita,*" Manuel agreed gravely. He lifted his cane and jabbed it toward the smoke. "My young men who are responsible for guarding our area have told me about them."

"Let me get this straight," Nolan growled. "A band of white men calling themselves Diablo are doing this? Why?"

"My sons—" Manuel began, then broke off as he looked warmly at the young men who were hustling to get the boxes off the Huey and loaded onto the truck. "Well…they are not really my sons, but that is what I call them." He looked at Rhona, his face growing gentle. "I have many sons and daughters here in our barrio, *señorita*. Perhaps not blood family, but a greater family, of the community."

"Yes," Rhona murmured, "I understand what you're saying."

"Of course you do. You're a very bright and alert young woman. You miss little." He smiled benignly. "My sons who patrol the edges of area six have talked to the people of area five, which is next to us. Yesterday they were told this gang of men were raiding and stealing food out of the mouths of children there. When the leader of area five refused to give them water and more food, they killed him at gunpoint."

"Damn," Nolan growled. Rubbing his chin, he studied the smoke. It was less than two miles from where they stood.

"That's awful," Rhona whispered. "And they're setting the fires to get even?"

"*Sí*, that is what we hear. If the people in the house do not give them food, then Diablo sets fire to their home and holds them at gunpoint so they cannot rescue anything from it. The family is forced to stand there and watch their place burn to the ground. This is so very sad. It is bad enough that the earthquake has us as prisoners. To have a gang of men with rifles going around and killing and hurting others...well, it is too much. Too much..."

Nolan saw the last box being removed from the Huey. He looked over at Rhona. Her face was sad, her gray eyes filled with compassion as she looked down at the old man hunched over his cane. When she reached out and touched his bent shoulder, Nolan felt his heart fill with such a powerful yearning he was caught completely off guard. What would her long, slender fingers feel like sliding across his own shoulder? Wonderful. And nurturing. Yes, that was it: Rhona was very maternal, very mothering and caring. That appealed strongly to Nolan.

His brows dipped. "We need to saddle up," he told her in a tight voice.

Rhona nodded and patted the old man gently. "We'll be back."

"*Sí*, and we are *muy*, much, grateful." Manuel smiled sadly. "Without you, without your help, the people of my barrio would die a terrible, slow death. Just know that this truckload of bottled water goes to our babies and into the mouths of our thirsty children...." With that, he stepped back and waved goodbye to them.

January 8: 0800

Rhona flew in taut silence. Nolan looked angry. And he moved restlessly in his seat as if he had ants in his pants. She didn't know what to make of that, because she didn't know him that well. Deciding to risk it, she spoke up. Within twenty minutes, they'd land back at Camp Reed and she might not get a chance to talk to him.

"What's bothering you?"

Nolan's mouth quirked. "I'm *that* readable?"

Chuckling, Rhona said, "You act like you'd rather

be anywhere than in this cockpit right now. You're restless.''

Sighing, Nolan rasped, ''I'm worried. Worried about that damned gang.''

''Is this something new going on?''

''Yeah, it is.'' He rubbed his chin and shook his head. ''I've got to talk to the major at Ops. There's got to be something we can do about this. I don't want those sons of bitches comin' over into area six. Señor Gonzalez looks out for the core of the barrio—where all the kids, the babies especially, are staying. They're trying to gather all the mothers and children together, where they can get them food and water. But if this gang goes in there...hell—'' Nolan broke off, frustrated.

''What about that marine squad that's going in? Aren't they supposed to supply law enforcement?''

''Yes, they are. But that's ten men—er, people— covering a two-square-mile area, on foot. You can't possibly keep everyone safe if there's a gang roving around.''

''The sergeant and his squad will probably set up a base camp and operate out of it, right?''

''Yeah, for sure. Probably in the core of the barrio, near where Señor Gonzalez has his house...or what's left of it. There's nothing left standing in the barrio. As you saw, everything was destroyed.''

Nodding, Rhona bit her lower lip. She guided the Huey onto the military reservation and began to drop altitude in preparation for landing. ''That's awful, what happened. Do you know who's flying into area five?"

"No, but I'll find out."

"Do they have any law enforcement there?"

"I dunno. Like I said, when we land, I'll make a call to Ops and see what I can find out."

He'd said "we" and not "I" this time, Rhona noted, feeling heartened. She saw him reach for the mike and call the tower for landing instructions. Heart singing, she hoped that his concern for the people would continue to outweigh her presence in his cockpit. From the worried look on Nolan's narrow face, she felt that with time, he'd adjust to her presence, and it would no longer be a big deal. Fervently, Rhona hoped that was true.

January 8: 0830

Rhona waited with the Huey as it was refueled and loaded, this time with MREs—meals ready to eat. She stood tensely as they were placed by the boxload onto the bird. Nolan had trotted over to the edge of the landing apron and gotten on the radio of a HumVee that was sitting nearby. The weather was growing worse. The wind was beginning to feel sharp to her, cutting through her lightweight, olive-green flight suit. The sky looked like it was going to dump rain at any minute. Marines hurried back and forth, responding to the threatening conditions. Everything seemed heightened and surreal. Rhona felt the tension. She couldn't escape it. Seeing Nolan leave the HumVee and start trotting in her direction, she felt her heart pick up in beat.

Nolan was a handsome man, there was no doubt. Rhona had noticed he didn't wear a wedding ring. Yet he was certainly old enough to be married. Did he have a wife and children? She suspected so.

The look on his face was grim. Her heart began to sink as he slowed to a walk as he approached her.

"This is crappy," he told her, pulling on his Nomex flight gloves.

"What is?"

"The situation in area five. I just found out that the Diablo gang has just killed the pilot and copilot in the Huey that was taking supplies into that area."

"Oh, my God," Rhona whispered. She saw Nolan's eyes go feral. His mouth was hard. "No…!"

"Yeah. I was just in touch with Lieutenant Mason. She's second-in-command at Ops. They're suspending flights to area five. They don't have a choice."

"But…the people there…" Rhona whispered. "They're being penalized because of that gang."

Nolan moved past her and made sure the cargo netting was secure. "Climb onboard, McGregor. We gotta turn and burn. I'll fly this time."

In a daze, Rhona climbed into the cockpit and strapped in. Automatically, like a well-oiled machine, they went through preflight procedures before Nolan fired up the engine and the blades began to turn. Once they were in the air, she spoke.

"What are we going to do? Is Camp Reed going to send in a squad to stop Diablo?"

Shrugging, Nolan said wearily, "Like we have extra marines sitting around with nothing to do?"

"I see...." Chewing on her lower lip, she asked, "Then what? What can we do?"

"Not much!" Nolan laughed, a sharp, hard bark. Off to their right, more and more columns of smoke were rising into the sky. That meant the gang was burning more homes of the helpless and needy. His anger rose. His hands itched, because if he could, he'd put his .45 to the bastards who'd killed those marine pilots. He'd do it in a heartbeat. They wanted a war? Well, they'd got one.

"You're going to tell Señor Gonzalez?"

"Of course. By the time we get there, another helicopter should have dropped off the squad of marines at the barrio." Nolan gave her a hard, quick look, then added, "We've been ordered, after we drop this payload, to fly over to area five and try to pick up that Huey."

Gawking, Rhona stared at him. "You mean...?"

"I mean we're to land, and one of us is to fly it home. We got clearance from the FAA to fly it out. If it's airworthy, that is. I hope the bodies of the men are onboard. If they aren't, Lieutenant Mason wants us to try and find them and get them onboard. Marines don't leave other marines behind."

The grim tone of his voice was like a knife sawing through her gut. "My God..." Rhona murmured.

"You sure as hell didn't volunteer for this kind of duty, did you?" Nolan gave her an assessing glance.

Taking in a huge, shaky breath of air, Rhona whispered, "I know I'm not a marine. I was in the navy. And I can handle myself in this situation, as ordered. If you're worried about me holding up my end of the deal—"

"I am," Nolan said frankly. "I'm finding myself seesawing here, worried that if anyone from Diablo gets anywhere near that Huey, they'll start firing at us. We don't have any ammo onboard except our pistols. They've got real firepower. I'm going to fly over the area and we'll assess it. If it looks like the Huey is free and clear, with no one around it, then we'll land."

She saw the fear in his eyes. Something else was eating Nolan alive. "I'll fly it back."

"Like hell you will."

"Why not?"

"Because..." He choked up for a moment. Getting ahold of his rage and grief, he whispered, "Because the guys onboard that Huey were good friends of mine. I know their wives...their kids. No, if anyone's gonna fly that bird outta there with them onboard, it'll be me."

Five

―――――――

Rhona tried to get comfortable on the unforgiving ground of the tent she'd been assigned to. It was 0100, and she was exhausted. The sandy earth, although swept smooth of pebbles, cactus and other vegetation, was hard and uneven. It was cold with the January wind buffeting the tent's closed flaps. Fortunately, the sleeping bag was a good one, made of goose down and nylon. For a pillow, she used her military jacket. On the other side of the small tent lay Nolan Galway.

One thing Rhona hadn't counted on was pilots bunking together. She'd mistakenly thought they'd be assigned to the B.O.Q., the Bachelor Officers Quarters. Silly her. She should have realized it would become a "hotel" for Logistics and Ops personnel who had to live, eat and breathe while keeping this entire mission moving forward twenty-four hours a day.

So much had happened today that her head was spinning. Although she was fatigued from twelve hours of flying, she couldn't sleep. Still clothed in her uniform except for the flak jacket, she moved onto her back, putting her hands behind her head and opening her eyes.

The tents the pilots slept in were staked out in three lines, with two feet of space between them. Now she understood more clearly why Nolan was upset at her being his copilot. It meant they ate, breathed and slept together in tight, cramped quarters, both in the cockpit of their Huey and in their pup tent. Keying her hearing, she listened to Nolan tossing and turning less than two feet away from her. He, too, was restless. Rhona knew why; having to fly the area five Huey with the bodies of two of his friends back to base would have gutted her emotionally, too.

Oh, Galway was a typical male, in that he shoved all his emotions deep down inside of him. But the rest of the day had been a special hell for Rhona while he sat stoically in the cockpit, more untalkative than usual. The few words he did utter were clipped, harsh. But all she'd had to do was look at his hard profile to know how much he was suffering and grieving.

Outside, she could hear the larger jets taking off and landing. The pilots' tent city was a quarter of a mile from the main airstrip. Every time a jet took off or landed, their tent shook and shuddered. How did anyone sleep? she wondered. And yet, right next door, Rhona heard the distinct snores of two male pilots. So someone was sleeping. Of course, they'd been pulling this grueling duty for eight days now, and this was only her first.

Rolling over on her side, she saw a sliver of light filtering through the front flaps of the tent. It made a jagged line down the center between their sleeping bags. A line of demarcation. The symbology wasn't lost on Rhona. Nolan needed to talk. He needed to get the grief, anger and whatever else he was feeling off his chest. Would he snap at her if she started talking to him now? Rhona knew he wasn't asleep.

Risking everything, she sat up, the sleeping bag pooling about her hips. As she settled her hands on her crossed legs, she heard Nolan sigh heavily. Bracing herself, she sat quietly, hoping he would engage in conversation.

"Can't you sleep?" Nolan groused irritably.

"No." Rhona tilted her head toward him. The darkness in the tent wasn't complete. With the sliver of light, she could just see his stoic profile. His hands behind his head, he was lying on his back, staring at the tent ceiling. Her heart beat a little harder when he slowly turned in her direction, his eyes glittering.

"Helluva day," he muttered to no one in particular, though he was very aware of Rhona. She was sitting up, her hands clasped in her lap, her hair loose and cascading beautifully around her lean, proud shoulders. Even in the dark, she looked beautiful. A huge part of Nolan wanted to simply turn over, crawl that two feet and find himself in her arms. He knew without a doubt from earlier today that Rhona had the compassion, the care, that he desperately needed.

"I feel like a Mack truck ran over my chest," he muttered, and lifted his hand to rub that area slowly.

"No wonder."

"No…" He swallowed hard. Closing his eyes, he rasped, "Dammit, I couldn't even make contact with the wives of my friends. The phone lines are down…. They live in Oceanside, in the same apartment building where I lived…and I can't reach them, can't tell them—"

Wincing internally, Rhona heard his voice crack with repressed emotion. To hell with it, she was going to follow her instincts. Rolling onto her side, she lay down and propped herself up on her right elbow. Reaching out with her left hand, she allowed her fingers to drape gently across his shoulder. Being this close, she could see the glitter in his eyes. From unshed tears, she realized as a poignant shaft of emotion jabbed her heart.

"I'm so sorry, Nolan," she whispered unsteadily, purposely using his first name. Her fingers dug a little more firmly into the shoulder of his flight suit. "Sometimes…sometimes just talking about it helps." She gave him a tender, unsure smile. He could round on her, bite her head off, she knew. Yet Rhona took the risk out of simple human compassion—and something else that lurked in the nether world of her swiftly beating heart. Holding his gaze, she felt the tension in his shoulder muscles. Rhona could feel the backlog of grief, like a huge water-filled balloon, surrounding him. Nolan needed to cry. But would he? He was a marine. And marines didn't cry no matter how bad it got. His hair was mussed, and several dark strands lay across his deeply furrowed brow. Her fingers itched to nudge them gently back into place. What Nolan needed was to be held. Nurtured. And Rhona could give him that as effortlessly as breathing; it came naturally to her. From the look in his narrowing eyes, he was surprised by her gesture, by her touch. Should she stop? Lift her hand away? *No,* her heart cried. *Keep touching him. It's helping.*

Obeying her instincts, which had never led her wrong, she continued on in a low tone. "I remember one mission during the Gulf War that I flew with my copilot. We got shot down by an Iraqi rocket."

Nolan scowled. "You took part in the Gulf War?" That instantly relegated her to a very high position in the military world. Any pilot who had seen combat was at the top of the pecking order. Combat pilots were the *real* warriors. They'd entered the gauntlet of war and survived. He felt the warmth and strength of Rhona's hand on his shoulder. Like a starving man, he was taking whatever she was giving him. Right now, he *needed* her touch, her care, whether he wanted to admit it or not. Just the look on her deeply shadowed face, that whiskey voice flowing over him like balm to his bleeding wounds, were soothing him, healing him.

"Yes, I was."

"What happened?"

Seeing his interest, Rhona eased down and rested on her outstretched arm. There was less than a foot between them now, her other hand still lying protectively on his shoulder. His eyes were alive with a new look in them—admiration maybe, or at least respect for her. That made her breathe easier. Maybe Nolan wouldn't bite her, after all.

"We crashed. Jake Turner, my copilot, was badly wounded. We were flying in supplies to a forward marine position that was up against the Iraqi Guard. My crew chief, Stephen Reardon, who was in the back of the helo, was killed instantly. I got a broken left arm out of the deal, so I was the least injured. Jake was in a bad way. The helicopter caught fire and I had to haul him out of his harness and out the back door, which had popped open in the crash. I remember lying between sand dunes with Jake in my arms, crying. I knew the Iraqis were around, and I knew they were coming for us."

Swallowing hard, Nolan listened with bated breath. Rhona really had seen combat. She hadn't just been a warm body waiting for orders. "What happened next?"

Opening her hand on his shoulder, she gave him a helpless smile. "I cried some more. Jake was bleeding to death, from a severed artery in his neck, and I couldn't stop the flow. I sat there and cried out of frustration and grief. I knew Jake's wife. I knew his two beautiful little girls. In the middle of that very cold night, Jake died in my arms. And I was angry. I hated what had happened. He was a good man, Nolan.

He loved his wife and worshipped those little girls of his. I hated what war had done to him…to my crew chief, who had just gotten engaged before we left for Saudi Arabia. I sat there in the sand, hurting so badly for Jake's family, and for Steve's fiancée.''

"Were you captured?" he asked in a low tone.

"No. When we were hit, Jake got off a mayday call, and we had a rescue crew come flying in about twenty minutes later, to pick us up." She sighed and gently smoothed some of the wrinkles from the shoulder of his uniform. Rhona could feel the tension flowing out of him. His face was less sorrowful. Tears still glimmered in his narrowed eyes, however. Maybe this was what Nolan needed to hear from her; she wasn't sure, but she kept following her heart.

"A marine Super Cobra had accompanied the rescue helo and made mincemeat out of the advancing Iraqis that shot us down. As we took off, it did my heart good to see that Cobra come flying by."

"It still didn't make up for the loss of Jake or Steve."

Shaking her head, she sighed, her hand once more coming to rest on his shoulder. "No, it didn't. When I got back to base, we had the capacity to call Stateside. I cleared it with the Defense Department and they agreed to let me contact Jake's wife, Ann, once they got the officers out to her house to let her know what had happened." Rhona closed her eyes and felt again those old emotions. Opening her eyes once more, she saw Nolan's eyes had an almost feral look in them. "I called her when I got the go-ahead to do so. I felt so bad, so guilty. I was the pilot in command. Why didn't I see that guard unit with the rockets? I cried with Ann. I told her how sorry I was, how frustrated and helpless I'd felt as Jake died in my arms. The only good thing to come out of it was that I was able to hear his last words. He told me to tell Ann that he loved her and the girls. At least I could relay that to her.''

"And then you called Steve's fiancée?"

"Yes," Rhona murmured, "I did. It was my responsibility to do that. I wanted to, anyway. I didn't want Patty to not know the truth of what happened— that Steve had died instantly. He didn't feel any pain, and that was good.'' Rhona gave Nolan a wry look. "I cried with her, too."

"Women always cry."

She chuckled softly. If she didn't pull back her hand, she was going to reach out and caress Nolan's dark, bearded face. His eyes were alive with grief. How badly he needed to cry for himself, for his friends and for the families who didn't yet know of their loved ones' fate.

"Yeah, it's a good habit we're trying to pass on to you guys."

Laughter rumbled up from his chest. Nolan forced himself not to react to her touch, to her care. Rhona's capacity to care, to reach out and touch his hurting heart, amazed him. It was as if she could see right through him and knew he was suffering deeply over the loss of his friends.

"I wish…I wish I could contact their families…."

There, it was out. Mouth thinning, Nolan felt her hand tighten briefly on his shoulder. It was enough. "I wish…want…to tell them what happened. They're over in Oceanside and they don't know a thing. They must be going through hell. There're no phone lines, no way to get hold of us, or vice versa. They don't even realize their husbands are dead—" His voice cracked.

Lifting his hand, he angrily swiped at his eyes, embarrassed by his display of emotion in front of Rhona.

"I have an ace in the hole, maybe," she said gently. "I have a friend, a very powerful friend, in Logistics. His name is Morgan Trayhern. Maybe if we can talk to Lieutenant Mason and get two relief pilots to fly our route for a bit, we might be able to get you what you need to reach Oceanside to tell the families. Are you game?"

Nolan sat up. He stared down at her. How soft and open her face was in the grayness. Her lips were parted…and kissable. The urge to take her in his arms and kiss her senseless moved through him, wiping out his grief momentarily.

"You can do that?"

"I can try, Nolan. No promises."

"Sure. That's great. If we could just try…it would mean a lot to me…to them. I'd be grateful."

Rhona smiled tenderly. "Come on," she urged, patting the ground, "lay down and get some sleep, Nolan. We're both blasted. We need at least five hours to keep going."

This time he lay down facing her, on his left side.

"You're right," he mumbled. Risking everything, he reached out and briefly grazed her hand with his. "Thanks...for everything. I think I can sleep now...."

January 9: 0600

"Rhona! How are you?" Laura cried warmly.

Grinning, Rhona stepped through the door of the hospital room. "Hi, Laura. I was over here on business this morning and thought I'd drop in and see you. I see you're well occupied." A bottle in her hand, Laura was feeding a baby girl swaddled in a soft pink blanket in her arms. Though her leg was still up in a cast, she looked better. The light blue nightgown she wore set off her fair features. Her hair was shining like gold coins, and she wore some makeup, which took away some of her paleness.

Chuckling, Laura said, "Oh, yes. I call this little one Kamaria. That's Swahili for 'beautiful like the moon.' Morgan has a good friend, a colonel in the army, stationed in an African embassy. His youngest daughter, who was born over there, has that name. When I met them, I was so taken with her beautiful name that I swore if I had another baby, and it was a girl, I'd name her after his daughter." She smiled fondly down at the infant in her arms. The child was suckling strongly, her huge blue-gray eyes looking up into Laura's with total trust and devotion.

Moving over to the bed, Rhona gently touched the baby girl's soft, dark hair. "That's a lovely name, Laura. I really like it." She smiled. "How are *you* doing? You're still trussed up like a Christmas goose here, I see.''

Rolling her eyes, Laura took a cotton cloth and, easing the bottle from the baby's rosebud-shaped mouth, gently blotted the corners, where tiny bubbles of milk had formed. ''I don't like being down like this, Rhona. You know me—always moving around. Can't stay in one place too long or too often.'' She chuckled.

''When do the docs say you can get out of this contraption?''

Making a face, Laura said, ''Not soon enough. I just suffered a blood clot in the area where they operated two days before you arrived, so they've finally got me on a blood-thinning drug, and want me to stay put at least another week before they even think of letting this leg down.''

Frowning, Rhona pulled up a chair and sat down. ''Bad news. But at least they found the clot before it moved, right?'' She knew a clot like that could kill a person.

Sighing, Laura eased the nipple of the bottle back into Kamaria's mouth. ''I know. Poor Morgan... He's beside himself with worry over me. I tell him to just go to Logistics and work, and I'll be fine over here. I have this beautiful baby to take care of, so I'm happy.'' She looked out the venetian blinds, through which the gray morning light filtered into the room. ''I'm a lot better off than most of the people out there. I feel so badly for everyone in this earthquake, Rhona.'' She turned and studied her friend. ''How are you doing?''

"Okay…" she lied, her voice softer than usual.

"You don't look okay."

"Caught red-handed."

"Again." Laura grinned and gently rocked the baby. "You were never any good at lying, Rhona. What's wrong? I can see it in your eyes."

"You're psychic," Rhona grumbled good-naturedly.

"Upon occasion. More a reader of body language, I think."

"Well—" she sighed "—here's what's going down…." And she told Laura everything. Just being able to talk out her fears, frustrations and problems with Nolan took a load off Rhona's shoulders. When she finished, she saw Laura frown.

"Will Morgan be able to get Nolan over to Ocean-side? There are no highways working anywhere in the basin area. He'd have to get a helicopter off the flight line to get him over there and back."

"Yes," Rhona agreed. "Morgan apparently has the connections, because once he heard Nolan's needs, he took him by the arm and said he could arrange the flight." She shrugged. "Morgan told me to come up here and keep you company. That Nolan would pick me up once he lands back here at the base after seeing the families of those two pilots and breaking the bad news to them."

Shaking her head, Laura watched as Kamaria's tiny eyes closed, her lips relaxing around the nipple as she fell fast asleep. Smiling gently, Laura set the bottle aside and dabbed at the infant's mouth one last time.

"Nolan is heroic. He cares. You're lucky to be flying with him, and that was wonderful of you to get him over here. Morgan usually can fix nearly anything that needs fixing." She glanced at Rhona and gave her a tender smile.

"Thank goodness he can. Morgan's pure magic, in my book. I'm glad he—and you—are here. I'm sorry you got hurt, but this place can use someone of Morgan's abilities right now. They need a master strategy advisor, and he does this every day with the fifty or so missions he has going at Perseus at any one time. Seems like he and his team are always dealing with some state of emergency. Morgan knows how to think on his feet, and he can develop a knee-jerk strategy that works. He's an excellent crisis manager. He's one of a kind, and I know the Marine Corps are grateful he's here helping them."

"Morgan's in his element, no doubt," Laura murmured, gently rocking the baby in her arms. "He loves what he does, Rhona. And he knows he's good at it. But enough of us. What about you? I see that every time you mention Nolan's name, your voice softens. You like this guy? Is he handsome? Single? A real twenty-first century kind of guy like Morgan?"

Laughing softly because she didn't want to awaken the baby, Rhona crossed her legs and said, "Don't go getting that look in your eyes, Laura. You're a matchmaker at heart and I know it. And no, Nolan Galway is just the opposite—a throwback to the Neanderthals. Yes, he cares deeply about his missions, like Morgan does, but he's stone age when it comes to accepting that a woman is as good as any man.''

''Ouch.''

''Yeah, no kidding.''

''You've had some pitched battles in the cockpit with him?''

''Yep.''

''Darn. Sorry to hear that. Still,'' she said, brightening, ''he doesn't seem *all* bad. Look what he's doing now.''

''I didn't say he was worthless,'' Rhona retorted with a grin.

''Is he married?''

''I don't know.''

''You don't know?''

''No, I don't.''

''Well, shoot. Ask! I think you kinda like him.''

Rhona chuckled, then sighed. ''Men don't like women asking personal questions of them—you know that, Laura. And yes, I do like him. But if he's married, I'll stop liking him and try to at least maintain a friendship, if I can even get that far.''

''Humph. I'll bet he's single.''

''Your intuition again?''

Grinning, Laura said, ''You bet.''

''Well, he's not going to be in a good mood when he gets back. I know what he's going to go through with those families. In some ways, he'll feel better, but in other ways…''

''Grief has its own time and ways of working out of each of us,'' Laura counseled her gently. ''And Nolan has you to confide in, whether he realizes it yet or not.''

Snorting, Rhona said, ''He'd just as soon confide in a rock. No, I take that back—he doesn't like to confide at all. Typical male, you know?''

''We'll see,'' Laura murmured sagely. She ran her fingers gently across Kamaria's tiny, smooth forehead and lifted several silky strands of dark hair back into place on her perfect little head. ''My money's on you to break this guy in right.''

''Like I want to,'' Rhona griped wryly.

Laura nodded, her smile disappearing. ''I understand. I'm so sorry your engagement worked out like it did.''

Rubbing her hands down her thighs, Rhona frowned. ''I'm glad it happened, Laura. At least the guy showed his true colors before I said 'I do.' I don't want to ever be stuck with a caveman. Not ever. I'll stay single and be glad of it, instead.''

''It's awful being lonely. I think everyone needs a friend, a partner. I wish every woman had a Morgan in her life.''

Rhona's lips lifted in a smile. ''Laura, if you could clone that man, you'd make billions selling copies of him, believe me. Yeah, I'm looking for someone like Morgan. He hasn't got a problem honoring women, and what they bring to the table. He believes in us, our smarts, our moxie, and the way we think and operate.''

''Yes,'' Laura murmured, ''he does. Well, listen, don't give up on Nolan Galway. My intuition tells me this guy isn't gold-plated, but he's gold on the inside. You might just need to get past all the outer rust on his armor to discover that about him.''

Chuckling, Rhona said, ''Forever the optimist, aren't you?''

''Do you like the other choice?'' her friend demanded archly, her blond brows lifting.

''Heck no. But I'm not sure about Nolan…''

''You'll find out a lot about him real soon,'' Laura counseled. ''You're going to be spending twenty-four hours a day with this guy for a while.''

''Yeah,'' Rhona griped, getting up and moving over to the window. ''I'll probably get to know him so well that I'll be sorry I wanted to in the first place.''

''Forever the pessimist.''

Placing her hands on her hips, Rhona turned and smiled at Laura, who was grinning hugely, like a cat who knew something she didn't. ''I prefer to think of myself as a realist.''

''I'm a realist with hope,'' Laura parried. ''You've just stopped hoping is all, Rhona.''

''I have good reason not to hope,'' she muttered, her brows drawing down.

''I know you do. You're still hurting from that broken engagement with Greg. But I think Nolan will heal that in you, if you'll let him. At least, that's what I feel.''

''You and your intuition.''

''Wait and see,'' Laura said primly. She rocked the baby gently in her arms.

''I won't have to wait long,'' Rhona said. ''I figure

Nolan will be back in another hour or two, and then we'll hit the flight line and put in our twelve hours today.''

"I'll bet he's not as unfeeling as you think him to be," Laura said.

Shrugging, Rhona walked back to her bedside and tenderly touched the baby's smooth, pink cheek with her index finger. "He has one crybaby in the cockpit already. Me. He isn't going to turn into one himself."

"Maybe this has taught Nolan that you're a safe person to reveal his feelings to," Laura said. "And with the danger to the helo crews out there now, well, there's nothing like a wartime footing to make you a very tight, tight team. No, I think he'll look out for you, just as you'll look out for him."

"War," Rhona whispered, her mouth flattening. She grazed the baby's soft hair. "You're right, Laura. The ante's been upped out there in the basin. This morning we heard that this Diablo gang is still in area five, but moving toward area six. I'm worried…really worried. Not for us, but for the people out there. They aren't armed properly to defend themselves against a bunch of civilians who have assault rifles and submachine guns. They're virtually helpless."

"There's a marine fire team of four people in place, though, right? That can afford them some protection."

"Yes and no." Rhona lifted her hand away from the baby. "Lieutenant Mason over at Ops got word earlier that Diablo is a lot bigger than we first thought. They've found out from interviewing people who live in area five that it's a group of adult males, all white, about thirty of them. They're heavily armed with assault weapons, grenades and all kinds of other heavy military hardware.''

"So, they're confirmed as survivalists and not just a gang?"

"That's the latest from Ops. Yes.'' Rubbing her brow, Rhona sighed. "You get thirty well-armed fanatics who want food and water and are willing to do anything to get it, and you've got a small war on your hands. And a marine fire team of four isn't going to stop them. Besides, area six is two square miles—a lot of turf to try and protect. The fire team has no mobility. They have to go everywhere on foot just like everyone else. There are no roads. The land's chewed up. Vehicles can't move anywhere.''

"I didn't realize all this,'' Laura murmured. "That's bad…and they're heading toward you…. Oh, dear, Rhona, you *really* need to be careful then.'' Laura reached out and gripped her hand. "I don't want you two shot in the head like those other pilots were.''

Grimly, Rhona said, "The mistake those pilots made was in trusting these guys when they came up to them.'' Her eyes flashed. "We won't make that error. Apparently, members of Diablo wear white headbands. That's a dead giveaway to us. So believe me, if we see some Anglo dude with a white headband coming toward us, we'll shoot first and ask questions later. No way are we going to be victims to bastards like that. No way…''

Six

Cursing softly to himself, Nolan tossed and turned in the darkened tent. How badly he wanted to crawl those two feet into Rhona's arms. Throwing his forearm across his eyes, he lay on his back and keyed his hearing to a C-141 jet that had just landed. The tent shook and shuddered from the turbulence as the pilot reversed the engines once it was on the ground.

That was how he felt: like a powerful aircraft in a brutal chokehold. Nolan was wild with grief, unshed tears, guilt and hurt. Why hadn't he just talked it out with Rhona today after he got back? Why? He was afraid, he admitted. Afraid of the soft look he saw in her eyes when he'd met her in Laura Trayhern's room after returning from Oceanside. Yet, wisely, Rhona had said nothing to exacerbate his raw feelings and chaotic state as they'd headed back to the flight line.

All afternoon and into the evening he'd wanted to somehow broach the subject, but didn't have the guts to do it. And in the chow hall, they'd sat across from one another, tense silence filling the void between them. Rhona, at least, didn't try to cover things with airy chatter. No, she knew he was stoved up emotionally, and she had the intelligence to back off and say nothing. It was up to him to open up. He couldn't expect her to pry like a can opener into his grieving, flailing heart. Automatically, he rubbed his chest beneath the goose down sleeping bag.

The ground was hard and unforgiving. Just like life was, he decided grimly. Focusing his hearing inside the tent, he felt soothed by Rhona's soft, shallow breathing as she slept. As soon as they'd come back from the chow hall and stumbled into their tent, reeling from exhaustion, she'd pushed off her black leather flight boots, crawled into her bag and slept— deeply.

Nolan didn't have the heart to wake her. She had flown just as much as he had today, and she was a workhorse behind the collective and cyclic. Nolan had been grateful for her professionalism in the clutch. Again he reminded himself that Rhona was a veteran. She had seen combat. He never had, so in the unspoken hierarchy among pilots, he was less a pilot than she was. That made him respect her despite the fact that she was a woman.

Snorting softly, Nolan removed his arm from his eyes and glared up at the grayish tent ceiling. The engines of the C-141 were now winding down to a warbling shriek as it made the turn at the end of the ten-thousand-foot runway. The craft would now trundle back to the revetment area, to have its insides disgorged by hardworking ground crews. Starlifters could carry more supplies than any plane in the military fleet, and Nolan knew that teams of marines would immediately attack, moving the goods to the helicopters that were now down for maintenance, refueling and resupply. At 0500, the pilots would get up, and by 0600, they'd be in the air once again.

Nolan turned toward Rhona, rolling onto his side. With a whispered sigh, he shut his eyes tightly. He *had* to talk to someone. He *needed* to talk to Rhona. Maybe tomorrow, in the cockpit, he'd try....

January 10: 0600

"You said Jake died in your arms," Nolan began when they were halfway to area six on their first run of the day. It was raining out, as if the weather gods sympathized with how he felt: the sky was crying the tears that were lodged tightly in his chest.

He saw Rhona glance at him out of the corner of her eye. "Yes...he did."

Quirking his mouth, Nolan muttered, "It musta made you feel really bad?"

Realizing he was trying to get to his own grief, Rhona put the clipboard down on her lap, her gloved hands resting over the cargo bill of lading that had the contents they were flying into area six. Nolan had asked to fly the first flight of the day. He'd actually asked—a huge change in his demeanor toward her since yesterday. It was a pleasant surprise that he was being deferential toward her today. It made Rhona breathe a sigh of relief. Nolan was treating her like a comrade, a team member instead of the "enemy." Rhona was more than grateful. "Yes…terrible. Like I told you before, I was sitting there sobbing and trying to stop the bleeding from that artery on the side of his neck. The thing was spurting blood a foot into the air, and nothing I could do would stop it."

"Felt pretty helpless?"

"Very." Rhona risked everything. "Is that how you felt yesterday? Going to see the families of the two pilots who were murdered?"

It felt like someone had stabbed him in the heart with an ice pick. Hands tightening on the collective and cyclic, Nolan rasped, "Yeah, I felt just like you—helpless. I felt so damned helpless, Rhona…."

Her heart surged with hope. He'd finally used her first name, instead of always calling her by her last name, which was typical in the military. Rhona decided not to say anything right away. She wanted to give Nolan the time and space to talk, if that's what he needed. Licking her lower lip, she watched the rain strike the Plexiglas windshield and slough off immediately because of their air speed. Their navigation software was still down and they had to do line-of-sight flying. The rain had cut visibility down to half a mile. At one-quarter of a mile they'd be grounded, because their helo lacked the instrumentation to fly safely in inclement weather. At three thousand feet, it was hard, even with their good eyesight, to locate the landmarks they normally used to find their way to area six. They were flying in iffy conditions, but neither wanted to be grounded.

"Pete's wife, Vickie, already knew." Nolan sighed painfully. "She had this awful nightmare the night before. We all lived in the same apartment complex, but now it's in shambles. The families are living like cave people over there…. They've gathered bits and pieces of roof, or siding, and made shelters out of it. When I found Vickie, and she saw me, she turned white. I thought she was gonna faint. The kids…" He grimaced. "Hell, it was awful. I stood there stuttering and stammering, my voice wobbling like a flat tire."

"Mine did, too, when I contacted my people's families," Rhona assured him gently. "They were crying at the other end of the phone line. I was crying at my end. It was hard, Nolan, and I'm sure no less hard than it was on you and the families you saw yesterday." Instinctively, Rhona reached out, laid her hand over his hard, tense forearm and squeezed gently. "You're a knight in shining armor in my eyes. You did the right thing." And then she forced herself to release her hold on him, because if she didn't, Rhona was afraid she'd be tempted to gather Nolan close and hold him. Hold him and rock him and help him eradicate that blackness jammed in his heart, which was eating him alive. She saw the grief in his slitted, forest-green eyes. And she heard it in his low, tortured tone the tears barely held at bay.

Rhona's touch was catalytic. Just the gentleness of her fingers, long and slender, wrapping around his forearm loosened the pain that was like a thrashing monster in his chest. The lump forming in his throat felt huge. He couldn't swallow. He could barely breathe now, and his eyes burned. Somehow he had to keep his mind on his job of flying this crate.

"When Vickie came to me, white as a sheet, and said, 'He's dead, isn't he?' I couldn't believe it. I just stood there in shock. All I could do was blubber yes, he was. His two kids—both no more than five years old—were wrapped around their mother's legs. I didn't want to tell her what had happened in front of them."

"No, of course not," Rhona whispered. She blinked her eyes, feeling his pain as well as the pain of those families. "And your other friend? Did you locate his family, too?"

"Yeah, they were on the other side of that trashed apartment complex, sharing with another family a few pieces of wooden boards as a shelter." Shaking his head, he said, "Janet didn't know. She didn't have a clue, but when I found them, and she saw me, she realized...."

"They always send out two officers and a chaplain to the wife or husband of a military person who dies," Rhona murmured. "How did she take it? Her kids?"

"Grab the controls, will you? I'm not seeing very well...."

Rhona slid the clipboard into the side pocket of her seat and wrapped her hands around the second set of controls. She glanced at him. His face was tight. She saw tears beaded on his dark lashes. Nolan was fighting with every bit of strength he had not to cry. "I've got the controls," she whispered.

Releasing his set, Nolan pushed back in his seat and pressed his helmeted head backward in an effort to take in a deep breath of air. His hands clenched and unclenched on his long thighs.

"Thanks…" he said, his voice cracking. Lifting his hand, he rubbed his eyes furiously. The shaking and trembling of the Huey felt comforting to him. Even more important, Rhona was near. Her voice, like velvet sliding over his tense nerves, was soothing to Nolan. Wiping his thinned mouth with the back of his hand, he stared ahead. Off to the left, the thick columns of smoke were being scattered by the falling rain.

"Janet was brave. Really brave, Rhona. They have three kids, two, four and seven. Janet just put her arms around all of them, held them, as I told her. She didn't cry."

"Military spouses are the bravest people in the world," Rhona agreed grimly. "They are made of very special stuff. They have to be in order to marry a guy or gal who's in the service. It's a career where every day could mean life or death, and they know it deep down in their hearts."

"Yeah…" Nolan shook his head and stared out the

side window of the cockpit for a moment. "I was married once, did you know?"

Rhona jerked slightly, then glanced at him. He was looking out the window, lost in the past. "Was?"

Giving half a laugh, Nolan said, "Yeah...Carol and I married when I came out of the Naval Academy. We'd been childhood sweethearts in Klamath Falls, Oregon, where I grew up. It was a dream come true for us—getting married and all. I had my whole life planned out." Nolan scowled and opened his right hand, then closed it into a tight fist. "Only Carol got breast cancer." He laughed without mirth. "All along, we were worried about me goin' down in a helo crash, or pulling duty somewhere and getting shot down...and she's the one who died instead. Helluva life down here, you know?" He closed his eyes, the hurt flowing out of him now that he'd finally released it. Somehow, Rhona was the right person to hear his darkness, his grief. Something in Nolan told him that she could handle it. She was a brave, steady woman who knew herself well. Rhona was no cream puff when it came to adversity. She'd handled combat, which said it all as far as Nolan was concerned. And she'd lived to tell about it, although he could sense that the wounds from that time hadn't healed completely yet.

"I'm very sorry about your wife, Nolan," she said. "How long ago?"

Sighing, he muttered, "Two years. She died just as I was getting transferred here to Camp Reed." Giving Rhona a sad look, he added, "Some days it seems light-years away and I can handle it fine. Other days…well, like yesterday…I have a tough time all around. I know what it's like to lose a loved one.''

"And yesterday it hit you like a sledgehammer.''

Shrugging, Nolan whispered, "Yeah, and I'm still reeling from it.'' He mustered a sad smile. "I'm not gonna be my normal sweet self in the cockpit today, so you might as well be warned now.''

"Not a problem,'' Rhona said, meeting his sorrowful gaze. She saw the grief that was eating Nolan alive. But there was nothing more she could do for him right now. In another ten minutes, they'd land at the baseball field. Señor Gonzalez would be there, as always, with his hardworking crew of young men and the old flatbed truck, to pick up their supplies and distribute them throughout the barrio.

"Were you…well…are *you* married?'' Nolan cringed as he asked that personal question, but he couldn't help himself. He needed to know. Seeing her cheeks color fiercely, he felt even more embarrassed over the intimate query.

Laughing unsteadily, Rhona said, "No, I'm not. Came close.'' She gave him a rueful glance. "I was engaged to this navy helo pilot about two years ago. Everything was going along fine, just hunky-dory, until he started trying to tell me what to do when we got married. Like marriage was a yoke and I'm the oxen pulling the plow?'' Derision filled her tone. "I didn't agree.''

"He had traditional values?'' Nolan guessed.

"Neanderthal values. And that doesn't sit well in my world."

"He wanted you barefoot and pregnant?" Nolan guessed, seeing the spark in her gray eyes. There was a slight grin pulling at the corners of her delicious mouth. How he was enjoying having her with him! And how he respected her since she'd confronted him on his prejudice toward her as a woman.

Laughing wryly, Rhona said, "Roger that one, loud and clear. Yep, Greg thought that I should just walk away from my career, marry him, be happy becoming pregnant and raising children. That was all I needed, according to him. Well, our engagement broke off at that point. He'd revealed his true nature, had finally come clean in the honesty department, and the life he'd mapped out wasn't a path I wanted to walk with him."

"But you loved him?"

"Sure, but you can love someone and not be able to live with them, too." She laughed sadly.

Nolan saw the hurt in her eyes. "It musta been a tough decision."

"Not really. I'm not giving my heart away to any man who won't respect me as a human being. It's real simple, Nolan."

"So, what made you leave the navy?"

"Greg and his squad mates," Rhona said. She brought the Huey to a hover, and they both checked out the rain-drenched baseball field below. Now, with the death of two marine pilots, everyone was under orders to hover and look over their landing area carefully before proceeding to land.

"They made it hard on you, right?" Nolan asked. He gave her a thumb's-up to go ahead and land the Huey. Off to the left he saw Señor Gonzalez and his young men waiting for them, umbrellas raised as they huddled together.

"Very hard. I took it for six months, then tried to get a transfer to another Sea Knight squadron that had fifty percent women pilots in it, but I got turned down. So I resigned my commission."

"Stupid move on the navy's part," Nolan growled. The Huey began to slowly descend from three thousand feet. The rain was easing up, but the sky was a gunmetal gray, with scudding white clouds like ragged ribbons on the far western horizon. From their vantage point, they could see the dark Pacific Ocean in the distance.

"Yeah, I thought so. But one door slams shut on your butt, another opens somewhere else." Rhona brought the Huey down, watching the altimeter. They were now at a thousand feet. She kept looking around, feeling jumpy about Diablo. There were no reports that they'd come into area six yet, but she wasn't going to risk being negligent about the matter. There was no way she wanted a bullet through her or Nolan's head.

"So, what opened up for you?"

"I'm half Navajo, from my mother's side. I've always been drawn to nature, and sound ecological practices. I love flying and didn't want to give it up. So I started my own crop-dusting company out in Bonsall.

I bought an older model Huey, retrofitted it for dusting crops, hung out my I'm Available sign, and have been busy ever since. Only I don't use herbicides and pesticides on farmers' crops. I use a biodegradable natural product from India, made with neem oil. It's an antifungal and antiviral oil that comes from a common tree over there. It kills every kind of pest you can think of, but doesn't poison the environment. It just washes off in the rain and returns to Mother Earth, in a nice, healthy way.''

The Huey landed as gently as a feather. Nolan continued to be impressed with Rhona's flying skills. He began to unbuckle his harness. "Let's finish this conversation on the way back," he said as he got up and slid through the narrow crack between the two seats. As he did, he brushed her shoulder with his hip. It couldn't be helped; quarters were tight.

"Roger that," Rhona said lightly, shutting down the engine and beginning to flip switches here and there across the control panel. Just the brush of Nolan's body against her shoulder sent wild tingles of pleasure up and down her arm. She felt happy for the first time in days. Nolan was proving to be a far better man than she'd ever hoped he could be. Laura Trayhern had been correct in her intuitions regarding him. Now Rhona looked forward to the trip back with him, and to the many long hours together in the days ahead.

Even though it was raining, the sky was a turgid green-gray, and disaster still escalated around them, Rhona felt a frisson of happiness she'd never experienced before. As she unharnessed, then headed toward the rear to help Nolan unsnap the nylon webbing around the cargo, she sighed. The day might be bleak, but to her, there was nothing but sunshine out there.

January 10: 0730

"So," Nolan said as they climbed to three thousand feet to begin their flight back to Camp Reed, "tell me more about this neem oil. It sounds like a great product that everyone in the world could use on crops instead of that poisonous stuff that's slowly killing all of us, getting in our drinking water and food."

Laughing, Rhona said, "You've hit the nail on the head, Nolan. That's exactly what neem oil could be. The neem tree is one of the most common trees in India and found everywhere on the subcontinent. Ironically, I stumbled upon it when I was back home, in Sedona, Arizona, when I went to a cousin's wedding." She gave him a grin. "My cousin married an ex-Recon Marine from Camp Reed—Captain Thane Hamilton. Small world, huh?"

"Yeah," Nolan murmured, rubbing his chin, "it sure is." The sky was lightening up, the rain beginning to ease off. He swept his gaze across the cockpit panel. At the speed they were going, the wind acted as wipers, removing the water from the Plexiglas.

"My cousin who got married, Paige Black, is a registered nurse at the local hospital. She found out about neem oil in a scientific paper that was printed up in one of the medical magazines. She gave it to me to read. At first, the oil sounded too good to be true, but over in India, people traditionally use neem on all their cuts and scrapes, or took it internally for parasite and worm infestations. It has a long, long history of saving lives when no modern medical drugs were available. So now the rest of the world is slowly discovering neem oil.''

"How did you decide to use it as a spray on crops?"

Chuckling, Rhona said, "I thought it up on my own. The paper said the people of India mixed the oil with water and poured it over plants in their gardens to save them from all kinds of bugs that would normally eat them up. I just extrapolated from that, wondering what would happen if I used it as a spray on hundreds or thousands of acres.'' Rhona shrugged and grinned at him. She saw the look of admiration on Nolan's face. "It worked. I've been doing crop dusting for a year, and the farmers who tried it, who risked their crops in my experiment, saw that it worked. Now I've got more business than I can handle.'' Her brows fell. "At least, until this earthquake came along.''

"That's pretty impressive," Nolan murmured. He liked the way her wonderful mouth curved in an elfish smile. What would it be like to kiss her? That thought had been hanging at the edge of his consciousness for over twenty-four hours. Was he ready for another relationship? He wasn't sure. Two years had passed since his wife had died. For the most part, the pain of his loss was gone, but never forgotten. Rhona was nothing like Carol, but that didn't stop him from liking her...or wanting her. Giving himself a mental shake,

Nolan pulled himself together. They were in a disaster situation, an ongoing crisis where danger and death surrounded them every hour of the day. And it would continue like this for months to come, he feared. He didn't even want to think about the people who were dying now...or those who would in future. It was just too daunting, too emotionally wrenching to accept. Now he understood, as never before, what it meant to be in a terrible disaster. They had always hit in other places around the world, never here. Until now.

So, he pondered, could he trust these feelings that were growing for Rhona? Was it the disaster causing him to feel this way? The unexpected and violent death of his two friends? Was it the inevitable camaraderie in the face of death and disaster that was drawing him to her? Or was it something else?

Unsure, he at least knew that he could no longer stop wanting her. And the way Rhona gazed at him—well, that soft, gray-eyed look of hers made him melt, made him yearn to be in her arms, to kiss her, to love her. Phew! The long hours, the sleep deprivation, the pressures were really getting to him. He had to be crazy.

Rhona kept her attention on flying back to the base. Still, in the back of her mind, she couldn't help thinking about Nolan. How he looked at her now, without the anger or prejudice he'd once felt. How his mouth was no longer tight with censure. Giddily, she tried to tell herself that she shouldn't be responding to him like that. He was a widower. She'd just broken off an engagement. What was real right now? Rhona wasn't sure. Feeling as if she were being tossed around emotionally like a tennis ball in a tournament, she decided to try and remain quiet and calm. Only, when Nolan looked at her, she felt a joy she'd never experienced before, and that jangled her, tempted and teased her as nothing ever had.

"So, you're half Navajo?" Nolan asked. "What's that like? I don't know much about Indians. My father is an auto mechanic who owns his own business back in Klamath Falls. My mother is a CPA and works out of their home."

"By any chance, are they Irish?" she chuckled.

Laughing, Nolan nodded. "Yeah. Can you tell?" He pointed to his long, lean face. "Black Irish is what my father calls me. I take after my mother's side of the family. They were potato Irish from around the Galway area."

"Not too far removed from the old country?"

"That's right. My father is an immigrant. I'm the first generation American over here."

"I like your Irish looks."

Warmth flowed up into Nolan's face. His grin was uneven and slightly embarrassed. "Thanks...I think."

"It gives you a very handsome look," Rhona assured him with a confident smile. "At least, in my eyes."

"Two compliments in a row. We're on a roll here," he murmured, very pleased with how she saw him. There was a pink flush on her cheeks, and her smile was shy.

"Maybe it's that Marine Corps thing, you know?"

she teased. "The few, the proud. I think you could be a poster boy for their print campaign."

"I'll call 'em up and tell 'em you said that." Nolan had a good gut laugh over that one. Inwardly, he preened with male pride at her assessment. She thought he was good-looking. He felt his heart warm at her words. Suddenly, he decided to share his humorous side with Rhona. Something told Nolan she had a great sense of humor, too.

"You know what President Reagan said about us?" Nolan asked, grinning.

"Uh-oh, here come some of those famous marine sayings." Rhona chuckled. "No. What did he say about you?"

"Some people spend an entire lifetime wondering if they made a difference. Marines don't have that problem."

Rolling her eyes, Rhona said, "Forgive your pride."

"Here's another really good one."

"Spare me, will you?"

"Naw, not a chance." He gave her a gleeful smile. The repartee between them was warm and alive. "To *err* is human, to *forgive* divine. However, neither is Marine Corps policy."

"*That* is true!" Rhona said. "Makes me glad I was in the navy."

"I've got a million of them." He waved his hand in excitement. "Marines are special."

"Yeah, you sure are," she replied, raising an eyebrow at him.

"Marines never die! They just go to hell and re-group."

Rhona held her stomach for a moment; it was aching because she was laughing so hard.

Nolan's expression turned serious as he said, "This thing going on in area five makes me recall a good saying. too. 'When in doubt, empty the magazine.'"

Rhona's own smile faded. "Yes, and even an ex-navy pilot will follow that wise Marine Corps order if we see any of those goons coming our way. I'm gonna shoot first and ask questions later."

Despite the reminder of the dangers of their situation it felt good to laugh a little. Black humor always raised its head when things got tense and dangerous. As she'd found out during the Gulf War, it just came with the territory.

Rhona felt heat stinging her cheeks suddenly. She glanced quickly in Nolan's direction. His eyes were warm...and inviting. Suddenly, the prospect of sleeping in that tiny, cramped tent with him became exciting and fearful at the same time. Could she trust herself with him that close to her? How badly Rhona wished she could reach out and snuggle into his arms. The world was deteriorating around them, coming loose at the hinges, tumbling out of control. Right now, the need for somewhere safe, someone loving, made her yearn keenly for Nolan.

Shocked at where her thoughts and heart were going, Rhona gulped. Quickly, she refocused on her flying. No matter what she did, however, the hot, burning coals of desire continued to glow within her. She'd had nearly a year and a half of sexual abstinence. And much to Rhona's chagrin, she was hungry for Nolan—in every way possible....

Seven

Nolan slept deeply that night, like a man who had for too long denied himself the luxury of falling completely into that dark, healing abyss. The moment his head hit the rolled-up jacket he used as a pillow, he was gone. In his dreams, which he normally didn't have, he saw Rhona. Her thick black hair was loose, flying around her shoulders like the ebony mane of a running horse. He was looking at her wonderful face, how broad it was, her cheekbones high revealing the Native American blood running through her. Now he knew why her skin was so golden. At first he'd thought she spent a lot of time out in the sun, getting a good, dark tan. How wrong he'd been.

In his dream, she was smiling at him with those warm, understanding gray eyes, and walking toward him. Her olive-green flight suit hung on her, camouflaging all her delicious womanly curves, but that didn't matter to Nolan. When she raised her arms, he stepped forward to take her in his. The moment her strong, lithe body met his, he groaned. She felt so damn good against him, and he could feel the strength of her, as her arms, firm and surprisingly strong, wrapped about his rib cage. The sensation was so real, Nolan could swear he wasn't dreaming. As he reveled in the sensation of her soft, warm breath against the curve of his neck, the pressure of her head coming to rest on his shoulder, and the tickle of her silky hair against his chin and lips, he sighed. He curved his arm around her and pulled her even closer.

In his dream, he felt the rise and fall of her small breasts against his torso. She was snuggling softly against his left side, her body melting into his. The sensations were electrifying, and heat surged through his lower body, jerking Nolan awake.

It was dark, except for the single shaft of grayish light from the airport coming in through the flaps of the tent. Lifting his head, Nolan felt heaviness against his left shoulder. Sleep fled completely as he lay back down. To his shock, he realized that sometime during the night Rhona had rolled over and into his arms. Lying there, Nolan blinked rapidly. In the distance, he heard another jet landing; probably a C-131 Hercules from the sound of the screaming, whistling turboprop engines. His awareness centered on Rhona once again.

Lying very still, unable to believe that this was real, Nolan realized his arms were around her. It was cold, he told himself. And very damp. Even now it was near freezing in their tent. Nolan told himself that she had probably gotten cold and unconsciously rolled over, seeking body heat to warm herself.

He was sure Rhona was asleep. He could feel her warm, moist breath moving like a wisp of a feather against his neck, where she'd pressed her face. Slowly lifting his arm from around her, he dared to do something he'd been itching to do for a long time—touch her hair. It was loose and free. He vaguely recalled that, as he'd crashed and burned the night before, she had sat cross-legged on top of her sleeping bag and released that thick ebony cascade. That was the last thing he saw before his eyes dragged shut from exhaustion after the day's harrowing events.

Holding his breath momentarily, Nolan realized Rhona's right arm was curved across his chest, her hand dangling on the right side of his rib cage outside the sleeping bag where he lay. How good it felt to have a woman's weight against him once again. Not daring to hope for anything other than this stolen, unexpected moment, Nolan raised his fingers and moved them very carefully through the strands of hair spread across his chest.

How strong and silky it felt slipping silently through his greedy fingers. How thick, healthy and clean smelling. Nolan inhaled deeply. Rhona felt so damned good to him—good enough to erase all the exhaustion, the stress, the danger. There was nothing like this, Nolan knew—holding a woman he loved in his arms.

His fingers froze in midair, the strands sifting and tumbling silently back to his chest. *Hold on.* He couldn't love Rhona. No, it was impossible. Love didn't happen this fast. Or did it? He'd known his wife all his life before marrying her after graduation from the Naval Academy.

Frowning, Nolan closed his eyes and eased his arm around Rhona once more. Just getting to lie here with her was a gift of such incredible value that he felt close to tears. Since his wife's death, he'd not been interested in women, in a relationship of any kind. And now Rhona came striding into his life, a woman warrior commensurate in skill to him. She was probably better than him, he admitted, because she'd not only seen combat, but survived it.

Was it possible to fall in love like this? Nolan lay there listening vaguely to the jets landing and taking off outside their tent. Relaxed and warm, as if still in a dream state, he tried to figure out what was happening. The urge to kiss Rhona was tearing at him. How many times had he wondered what it would be like to kiss her shiny blue-black hair? Or seek that soft mouth of hers, which flexed with every emotion revealed in her rabbit-gray eyes?

He felt Rhona's body jerk suddenly, as if she'd been electrified. Tightening his arms around her, he felt her tense up. A moan slipped from her lips.

"Shh," he whispered unsteadily, his mouth pressed against her frowning brow. "It's okay, darlin'…you're safe. No one is gonna hurt you…you're safe. You hear me?'' His voice drifted off into the night, absorbed by the sounds of the eerily shrieking jets.

Almost instantly, Rhona relaxed. He felt her take a shuddering breath into her lungs, and then release it in a warm, moist flow across his neck and shoulder. His voice had calmed her. Had soothed her. Amazed by it all, Nolan lay there feeling like a man who had been granted one last dying request before he went to the gallows. This was an extraordinary woman in his arms. She was all warrior, but still so feminine. He couldn't quite make the two mix in his mind. At least, not yet. Nolan had never wanted to think of any woman as a warrior like himself—he supposed because he felt threatened by the possibility. Yet Rhona was his equal in every way, and he no longer felt threatened by her. If he was honest with himself, he would admit he admired her greatly, his respect for her building hourly. There was nothing to dislike about her, Nolan decided. She was a plus in every way.

His heart began to open, and the feeling was very real to Nolan. It was as if his heart were a tightly closed rosebud that now, petal by petal, was opening up in his chest. The joy that came with it was new to him. It stymied him. What was the cause of this happiness that almost made him want to laugh out loud, to dance? A ribbon of sunlight wrapped around his heart, and the intensity of his feelings toward Rhona left him stunned and breathless in the wake of his discovery.

There was no denying any longer that he was interested in her. Yet Nolan was scared. He'd lost one woman he'd loved. Deep down, he knew he was a coward. There was no way he could reach out emotionally and love any woman again because the cost of loving was simply too high a price to pay. It had taken two long, nightmarish years to put his grief over his loss behind him. And now this woman who lay trusting and asleep in his arms was snagging his heart and opening it. Asking him to reach out and love again.

Closing his eyes, Nolan took in a ragged, painful breath of air. Something bade him to kiss Rhona. At least kiss her once. Yes, that was all he would need: one stolen, chaste kiss. Aching to feel her lips against his, Nolan rose carefully up on his left elbow, cuddling her head against his arm. The thin, weak light revealed her to him as he lay on his side, absorbing her vulnerable features into his starving heart.

Moving a thick strand of hair off her cheek, Nolan fought within himself. It wasn't right to kiss her without her knowledge. She would wake up. And then what? Slap him? Get angry? Rightfully so, he realized. His brows drew downward. No, this wasn't right. He could taste her—but not this way. He wanted Rhona badly, but not like this. She had to want to kiss him as well. Right now it was one-sided, and that wouldn't work.

Easing back down, Nolan continued to lie on his left side. He brought Rhona gently against him once more, closed his eyes and spiraled into sleep. This time it was dreamless, but the knowledge that she lay in his arms was all he really needed for now.

January 11: 0500

Rhona awoke slowly. She stretched, luxuriously, because she felt warm and safe. As she moved her arm, she realized drowsily that she was lying against something. Pulling her eyes open, she could barely see anything in the weak gray light of dawn. The tent shook as a jet landed. Where was she?

As if in a delicious dream, Rhona looked up…and realized with a start that Nolan was not only awake, but looking down at her with a hooded warmth lingering in his smoky green eyes—warmth toward her. And then, as she slowly came awake, Rhona realized she was lodged right up against him, from head to toe. One corner of Nolan's mouth was hitched upward, but he wasn't laughing at her. No, the look in his eyes told her he wanted her as a woman—that he wanted to lean across those scant inches that separated them and kiss her.

Rhona's breath caught. She had been sleeping against Nolan. For how long, she didn't know. What she did realize was that sometime during the night, she'd found her way over to his side of the tent. Embarrassment flooded her, and yet her heart was beginning to slowly pound in anticipation. Nolan wanted to kiss her. She'd recognize that look anywhere, despite the fact that right now, her mind was fuzzy and half-asleep.

She was never any good the first hour after waking up. It was tough to put things together right now. How had she ended up here? In his arms? Mind spinning, Rhona realized that he hadn't pushed her back to her side of the tent, either. No, his left arm was beneath her neck, cradling her head. And his right arm was stretched across her, his hand resting firmly on her hip to keep her close to him. Stunned, she lay there looking up at him, speechless. So many wonderful emotions spilled out of her heart toward him. The look of a predator lingered in his eyes. Nolan wanted her. All of her.

Those realizations shot through Rhona like a bolt of lightning. She lay there barely breathing, snared by his glittering green eyes. Her gaze moved slowly downward…to that strong, male mouth curved boyishly in a slight, one-cornered smile. It wasn't a smile that said *I've got you*. No, it was a smile of welcome—welcoming her into his arms to share this exquisite moment that neither had expected or conspired to create.

Her feelings running rampant, Rhona ached to reach out and kiss him. The invitation was there. Nolan wanted her. Did she want him? Yes. Yes, she did. In the worst way. There was something primal about Nolan, and yet at the same time he made her feel safe. Safe. No man had ever made her feel like this, until now.

Suddenly all the reasons why she shouldn't kiss him, why she *should* back out of his arms and give him a lame apology, exploded within Rhona. Yet as she drowned in the warm invitation burning in his green eyes, all those thoughts dissipated. Rhona was afraid. She'd sworn never to fall in love with a man from the military again. After her last painful experience, she'd never even wanted to look at another one—until Nolan came waltzing brazenly into her life, rocking her steady world. Oh! How many times in the cockpit did she steal a sly glance at his rugged profile and want to kiss that mouth of his?

Well, here was her chance. Should she take it? What would the cost be? Rhona groaned inwardly. Sometimes she wished her mind wasn't always counseling her and she could simply listen to her heart, which was pumping powerfully with joy right now.

Throwing all her cautiousness out the door, Rhona lifted her hand, sliding it up the side of Nolan's jaw. Her fingertips prickled because he hadn't shaved yet, and the sensation was wonderful to her. His eyes became slits. His arm tightened around her, claiming her.

Lips parting, Rhona whispered, ''Nolan…I'm afraid….''

His smile deepened as he caught her hand, turned it over and pressed a warm, lingering kiss into the palm. ''So am I, darlin'. Scared to death.'' And he lifted his head and gazed directly into her eyes.

Nolan saw the desire for him in her wide gray eyes. It made him feel good and strong as a man. Rhona was his equal, and it was so exciting and new to be with a woman who was his true equal that he forgot his normal hesitancy. Tucking her hand between them, her palm against his chest, he whispered, ''Let's be

scared together...." And he leaned down...down, to
seek and find her lips.

Moaning softly, Rhona shut her eyes and lifted her
face to meet his descending mouth. *Yes.* This was the
most right thing in the world to her in a world gone
mad. His lips brushed hers tentatively in that scalding,
heated moment, then moved with slow deliberation
across hers, tasting her, feeling her, exploring her. He
was introducing himself to her.

Nolan's kiss was agonizingly, beautifully slow as
he ran his tongue across her lower lip. Rhona sighed,
pressed herself wantonly against him to let him know
how much she wanted, needed him, woman to man.
She felt him smile against her opening lips—a very
male smile filled with confidence and certainty. Her
heart exploded violently with long-held emotions. As
his mouth claimed hers in a swift, urgent coupling,
she moaned and surrendered herself in all ways to Nolan.

The moment his mouth captured hers, Rhona's tidy
little world shattered around her. She felt his strong,
lean hand move confidently down her spine and come
to settle against her hip. Even though the sleeping bags
were bunched between them, she could feel his need
of her as he brought her hard against his hips. Her
breasts pressed against his well-sprung chest. Sliding
her arm across his torso, Rhona pulled Nolan tightly
against her. Their mouths were hungry, obsessed, their
breathing ragged and on fire.

As his left arm lifted her head upward, to position
her more fully against his hungry mouth, Rhona felt

as if she were heated water flowing against the hard rock of Nolan's body. Her skin tingled wildly where his breath flowed across her cheek. As his hand slid upward, ranging across the thick folds of her sleeping bag and grazing her covered breast, which was taut with need, she moaned. For a moment, her mouth separated from his, but not for long.

"Come here," he whispered darkly, seeking her wet lips once more.

His voice vibrated through her. Dizziness swept Rhona as he rocked her lips open, plunging her into a scalding vat of boiling desire. Heat flooded her lower body. Aching to have him, to claim him in every way, Rhona released the last of her hesitation. Every second of life was precious. Every second should be lived. She'd heard that so many times from her wise Navajo mother. For in the next second, life could be ripped away, and a person would never know what was lost through hesitation. Yes, life was to be lived in the moment. Well, she was going to do that now, with Nolan.

The moments spun like superheated fragments of red-hot lava violently exploding out of a volcano as their seeking, searching mouths devoured each other. When his hand ranged up to her face, his strong fingers brushing her cheek, Rhona wanted to cry at the tenderness of his gesture. Nolan was commanding, strong, and yet at the same time incredibly gentle with her. He wanted her participation, coaxed it out of her, and together they enjoyed one another in a way she'd never experienced before with any man.

Slowly, agonizingly so, Nolan pulled away from Rhona's warm, hungry mouth. He didn't want to break off their kiss, yet knew he must. Somewhere in the back of his mind, he realized they were late getting up. And if they didn't stop...

"We've got to stop," he said huskily against her mouth, kissing her one last time...and aching to do so much more than just that with her. Opening his eyes, he drowned in Rhona's slumberous gaze. The urgency to love her thoroughly, to claim her savagely as his woman, was nearly Nolan's undoing.

"I don't want to...but we've got to," he rasped, his voice unsteady. Sliding his fingers through her unbound hair, he drew away from her slightly. Rhona's cheeks were suffused with a rose-pink flush, her breath coming quickly, her lips parted and begging him to kiss her one more time. Nolan didn't dare, or he'd strip her out of that sleeping bag and take her. Now. Here. And to hell with the reality of what lay outside the little tent they shared. A huge part of him wanted to throw responsibility out the door, but he knew he couldn't. Not yet...not now.

"Y-yes," Rhona quavered. She tore her gaze from his. "I don't want to, but I will...."

Laughing a little, Nolan released her so that she could sit up and move back to her side of the tent. Her hair tumbled down around her shoulders like a wild ebony brook. Aching to love her, he sat up and simply watched as she raised her slender hands, sliding her fingers through those tresses to tame them into some semblance of order.

Looking at his watch, he said sadly, "It's 0520. We're going to be late if we don't get on it. We're due at Ops at 0545...."

"I know," Rhona murmured, fumbling for the small plastic case that held her brush and comb.

"Wait...." Nolan reached out as she gripped her toiletry case. His hand closed over her arm and turned her toward him. Her eyes widened with surprise at his unexpected gesture.

"I'm not sorry this happened, Rhona," Nolan said in a deep voice. "I just want you to know that...." And then he released her. Nolan didn't want to, but to touch her was like getting burned, consumed with a flame of desire that ate him alive. He watched the blush deepen on her cheeks. Her lashes moved down and she hung her head for a moment. And then she lifted her chin and looked at him.

"I'm not sorry either, Nolan."

Nodding, he managed a thin smile. "Good. You know, I woke up hours ago, thinking I was dreaming of you in my arms, and you were really there."

Rhona wanted these precious few minutes with him, wanted to talk honestly and privately. But time was pushing them. People were thirsty and starving out there, and she knew she and Nolan had to get moving soon. Breathless, she whispered, "I must have turned over in the night. I was cold...."

"I know."

"I didn't even realize I'd done it...."

"I'm glad you did. Maybe we're all more primitive

than we realize." He grinned slightly. "The cold made you seek warmth. Me."

Managing a strained laugh, Rhona unzipped her toiletry case and quickly ran her brush, and then her comb, through her hair. A wolflike look came to Nolan's eyes as he sat there watching her. "I can't explain it," she murmured, embarrassed. "I don't even remember doing it."

"I kinda liked it."

Rhona paused, her comb suspended above her head momentarily. In the grayish light, Nolan's face was carved with light and shadow. The darkness of his unshaved face gave him a new, dangerous quality that made her heart skitter. He would be a strong, wonderful lover, she knew. The hunger and need for that kind of care, that kind of love, was nearly her undoing.

"I did, too."

"You don't play games, do you?"

She put the brush and comb away and quickly took out the pins to put her hair into a French roll. "No, I never did."

"Neither do I." Nolan shrugged. "Maybe because I had a sweetheart from high school on, and then married her, I never got into game playing."

Putting the finishing touches on her hair, Rhona reached down near the flap of the tent and grabbed her unlaced flight boots. Nolan was doing the same. He felt the responsibility of time, too, and knew they had to get to the revetment area to fly their first load of supplies out on schedule. Their personal life, their needs, were strictly secondary to the disaster around them. A fierce emotion, one Rhona was afraid to name, swept through her as she watched him slide out of the sleeping bag and put his boots on.

"We need to hurry," she said, unzipping her own bag. "Maybe we can talk more during the flights?"

"Yeah," Nolan said, lacing up his boots with a familiar expertise, "I'd like that, Rhona." Then he pinned her with a look that made her freeze. "I'd like to know about you, the woman. About your growing up years, your life…."

Mouth dry, Rhona stared at him. Forcing herself to move, she quickly grabbed her flak jacket, which she had folded and put in a corner of the tent. Fear galvanized her. Was she ready for a relationship? How could she be? Her heart was leaping with such joy she could barely think straight. And yet she was afraid to put a name to what she felt toward Nolan. He was a marine. She'd already had the worst wounding of her life from a military pilot. Could she afford to try again? Rhona wasn't sure.

Her hands shook as she laced her boots. Fear took over. The time to live life in the moment had come and gone. Did she have the courage it took to reach out and try again? And how could she be feeling so much so fast? Nolan had fought with her from the day they'd met, and now they'd just enjoyed the most beautiful, tender kisses Rhona had ever shared with a man.

What was happening? Her well-ordered world was suddenly tumbling out of control. The earthquake had shattered much of it. And now Nolan's hot, caressing mouth had completely dismantled her heart and soul.

Eight

The sun coming through the Plexiglas was bright as they flew back from area six on their first mission of the day. Nolan had asked her to fly, and Rhona reveled in the new energy that pulsed between them in the cockpit. Ever since those breath-stealing, soul-feeding kisses this morning, she couldn't stop happiness from bubbling up in her heart. And judging from the lessened tension on Nolan's darkly handsome face, Rhona realized that the kiss had been healing for him as well. The relaxed atmosphere in the cockpit was new and welcoming. This was the way it should be between pilot and copilot; there was an ease between them, a space where they could both let down their guard despite the strains and stresses going on around them. They could rely on and trust one another.

Nolan finished writing a report on the clipboard on his knees. He looked up and smiled at Rhona. "Señor Gonzalez looked pretty happy this morning, didn't he?"

Just the warmth in Nolan's voice sent a thread of desire vibrating through Rhona. Glancing briefly in his direction, she smiled back at him. How wonderful it was to smile with Nolan! "Yes, he was. That first load was medicine, and they have some very sick people who desperately need the supplies we gave them."

"It's surprising how much the basics of life mean when you suddenly have them all taken away, you know? You can't pick up the phone and call a doc now. Or call in a prescription. No phone lines. No way to get to the doc even if you had a phone." Shaking his head, Nolan placed the aluminum cover over the clipboard and stowed it behind his seat. All he wanted to do was look at Rhona, absorb her into his joyous heart and singing soul. Her eyes were tender and vulnerable this morning—more than ever before—and Nolan felt grateful. He was going to try and take care not to hurt her or make her close up, as he'd done in the past.

"Even the few homes left standing are too unsteady to enter. And it's dangerous to climb into the rubble to try and find even a bottle of aspirin," she agreed sadly. The day was dawning clear and bright. It was cool outside since the front had come through, and the sky pale blue and cloudless. Thankfully, she could drop her dark visor to shield her eyes from the strong rays of the rising sun on the eastern horizon.

She glanced at Nolan once more. His profile was strong and clean. And his mouth… She sighed inwardly. All she could think about was kissing that mouth of his again. Gently, Rhona pushed those thoughts away, because they had no business here in the cockpit. Flying was a full-time job. She couldn't afford to be daydreaming.

"Did you hear Señor Gonzalez talking about his daughter Consuelo?" Nolan asked. "She's pregnant."

Shaking her helmeted head, Rhona moved her gaze across the control panel. "No, I hadn't heard. Is everything okay with the baby?"

"Are you having some kind of woman's intuition?" he asked, surprised at her insight.

"About what? Is she in trouble with the pregnancy?"

"She's eight months along. I guess she's having labor pains and it's too soon. Señor Gonzalez asked me if we could take her to Camp Reed."

"The hospital is overflowing with patients," Rhona said.

"Yeah, it's a damned if you do and damned if you don't situation."

"You look like a man with a plan, if I'm reading you right," she said, her gaze flickering briefly toward him. She chuckled.

"Yeah, I'm hatching a plan as we speak," he said pensively.

"Well," Rhona replied teasingly, "I'm not going to be the one to say you can't scheme, Galway."

"Yeah, I schemed to get you and look what happened," he said provocatively. Watching Rhona's cheeks color, he squelched the very real urge to reach out and brush her skin gently. She was bringing out that tender, vulnerable side of himself, but with her, it felt good. And more surprising, he felt safe doing it.

"*You* schemed," she snorted, laughing. "Remember? It was me who rolled over in the night, unawares. You didn't haul me into your arms, Lieutenant. I came over to *you*. Gosh, you've got an awfully short memory. Is that because of your male pride? Or were you having a senior moment? Hmm?"

Nolan chuckled, enjoying bantering with Rhona. She was sharp and thought on her feet. Rubbing his jaw, he watched the ground far below them. As always, the shuddering of the helo felt good to him, like a mother's arms rocking him. "Well, maybe I did have it all wrong. You did the scheming, it seems...."

Making a squawking noise of protest, Rhona tipped her head back and laughed deeply. "Let it not be said you can't play the game like a pro!" She chortled.

"Do you know how beautiful you are?" The words came flying out of his mouth. He saw their impact instantly in Rhona's face. She gaped at him momentarily, caught herself, then devoted her attention strictly to flying.

"More Irish charm by the gallon being dolled out here, Galway?" she teased. He thought she was beautiful. Her heart mushroomed with such happiness that

Rhona didn't know what to do. For the moment, all she could manage was sitting in the seat and absorbing his husky compliment. Then she remembered the look she'd seen in his eyes when he'd said the words—those eyes, those eyes that spoke so eloquently. Green, narrowed and filled with desire—for her. Gulping, Rhona felt tongue-tied. She was twenty-eight years old! She shouldn't be feeling like an uncertain teenage girl.

"Ahh," Nolan whispered wickedly, "my Irish charm is more than just word games, darlin'." Enjoying the high blush that stained her cheeks a soft red, Nolan reached out and slid his hand across her shoulders for just a moment.

The friction of his gloved hand gliding caressingly across the top of her flak jacket created a tingling sensation. Once he moved his hand away, she saw him sit back in his seat with a smile that was pure male. Obviously he was very pleased with himself and how he affected her.

Trying to think clearly, Rhona said, "When I was a little girl, growing up on the Navajo reservation, I used to go to this one red, sandy hill. I'd lie on my back, my hands behind my head, and just watch the white clouds pass above me."

"Sounds like a nice pastime," Nolan murmured. He was starving to learn more about Rhona, and now she was going to gift him with more information. The tone of her voice had dropped to a more intimate murmur.

"I used to see shapes in the clouds. A coyote. A snake. A rabbit. And always, I wanted to be free, like the ravens that fly over the res, up there among those clouds' spirits.''

''So, you've wanted to fly since you were a little kid?''

''Yes. My Navajo mother used to tell my father, who is an Anglo, that I should have sprouted wings instead of arms.'' Rhona chuckled, remembering those days.

''I guess we're a lot alike,'' Nolan murmured, watching the sun's long shadows stretch over the land beneath them. ''My dad loves to fish and we'd go to Klamath Lake, right outside the town where I grew up, and he'd sit on the shore for hours, dipping that pole of his into that cold, blue water. I'd take off and try and scare up the shorebirds and ducks, just to watch 'em fly. I envied them. There was a great blue heron rookery at one end of the lake, surrounded by walls of cattails, and a small knoll above it. I used to climb the knoll and watch them fly in and out.'' He glanced over at her, absorbing the sight of her soft, parted lips. Lips he wanted to capture and tame beneath his. ''I wanted to be like the great blue.'' He sighed. ''I didn't like being earthbound at all. I knew my freedom was up here.'' And with a jab of his thumb he motioned to the sky that surrounded them. ''Turns out that's when I'm happiest—when I'm in the sky, flying.''

''What about your marriage? Didn't being with your wife make you as happy?''

Nolan considered her question. Opening his gloved hands, he looked down at them. ''Being married was equal to flying, Rhona. Not that it was a perfect marriage, but the thing we had going for us was we were best of friends, too.''

"Besides being in love?"

"Yes." He turned his hands over and rubbed them slowly up and down his thighs. "Maybe because we grew up together, went to the same schools…I don't know. But I liked having her as a friend *and* a lover.''

"I don't see that happen often in a marriage," Rhona said, frowning.

"Maybe that's why so many of them break up. Because they're based on sexual attraction only. Maybe what happens is that when the newness wears off, there isn't anything substantial left to hold the marriage together and have it move forward from there."

"You're right," Rhona agreed fervently. "When I was engaged, my relationship seemed to have all the right stuff, or so it looked. But when it came right down to it, he wasn't a friend. He wasn't someone I could confide in and trust. It was all sex."

Nolan shrugged. "I think most of us go through that. I didn't, but I see it being played out around me all the time."

Sighing, Rhona said, "I just wish I'd realized that before I got engaged. I *should* have."

Laughing heartily, Nolan slapped his knee and said, "Oh, you and millions of others." Reaching out, he squeezed her shoulder momentarily. "Hey, don't be hard on yourself, darlin'. That's called life. The key is to learn from your mistakes so you don't commit them again."

She nodded and pursed her lips. She wanted to say, *But our relationship is pure sex, too. Where does that leave us? Will there be anything but sex to build on after we reach that plateau? Can there be friendship?* But she knew that it was too soon to know which way things would go.

Rhona focused on their upcoming approach to Camp Reed. Nolan got on the radio and received landing instructions as well as clearance. Below, off to their left, the long black asphalt runway was stacked to the gills, literally, with all kinds of incoming and outgoing aircraft.

"Man," she whispered, "I would not want to be an air controller in that tower. It must be murder to keep all this traffic straight."

"No kidding." Nolan glanced at her. Her face was set and serious. "I think we'll opt for flying, not being tin pushers."

Chuckling, Rhona agreed. "Pushing tin" was an axiom that air controllers used for what they did. The "tin" was an aircraft, and they "pushed" it from one point to another on the radar screen.

"What's up on this next flight?" she asked. Nolan had the manifest for the cargo they'd fly today during the twelve-hour mission.

Pulling out the clipboard from behind his seat, he flipped open the lid and ran his finger down the lines of type. "MREs. Food."

Nodding, Rhona brought the Huey down for a landing. "Good. Señor Gonzalez was saying they're really hurting for food. He worries me, Nolan. That old man is so thin and frail. One of the young guys said he's giving half his rations away to others.''

''Yeah, he's losing weight,'' Nolan muttered as he felt the Huey gently kiss the landing apron. Once again he admired Rhona's wonderfully light touch with the helicopter. The same kind of touch she had with him.

Shutting down the engine, Rhona unharnessed herself and got ready to disembark once the crew chief opened the fuselage door. ''He's so frail, yet so strong in spirit. You see it in his eyes. He cares for his people. Those boys—young men—who work with him just idolize him.''

Nolan released his own harness. ''Yeah, he's a saint in their eyes. And a wonderful leader in a mess like this.''

''Do you think we can do anything for his daughter?'' Rhona saw the rear door slide open. The crew chief saluted her, and she lifted her hand and saluted back. It was time to get out, go to the head, grab something to drink or eat, and then hurry back to the helo once it was loaded up for the next flight.

Nolan motioned for her to leave the cockpit first. ''Yeah, I've got a card up my sleeve….''

She squeezed out between the seats and then jumped out of the helo. Once on the tarmac, she waited for Nolan to join her. Already the crew chief and his team were beginning to prepare the aircraft for another load of cargo.

Settling his dark green garrison cap on his head, Nolan walked with Rhona toward the edge of the landing apron. They kept closely together, their shoulders and arms occasionally touching. Around them, the place was a mad chaos of controlled activity with people, HumVees and diesel trucks everywhere. On top of that, there was the continual whine and shriek of aircraft engines and the whapping of helos coming and going. The level of noise was constant and earsplitting. Waiting until they got to the tent area, Nolan reached out and stopped her.

Turning, Rhona faced him. The sun made her squint, and she took the aviator sunglasses from her left pocket and put them on. There was a slight, cooling breeze, and the sun felt warm and good as she stood near Nolan.

"Listen, I'm gonna go over to Ops and talk to Lieutenant Mason."

"Okay...I'll get us breakfast boxes from the chow hall and meet you back at the Huey?"

Nodding, he said, "That's a roger." And he turned and headed for the three-story concrete building in the distance.

January 11: 1100

Rhona had disembarked from the Huey once they'd landed back at area six, and followed Señor Gonzalez, who had brought his ailing daughter to the field. As they approached the gold-colored sedan where Consuelo waited, far from the activity on the field, Rhona glimpsed the dark-haired woman sitting in the passenger seat.

Rhona had just stepped up to the side of the car so

Señor Gonzalez could introduce her to his daughter when she felt something was wrong. Straightening, she frowned. A chill worked up her back. Turning toward the helo in the distance, she studied it for a moment. And then icy fear gripped her. All movement had stopped at the Huey. Why? Blinking, she took off her sunglasses and narrowed her eyes. Rhona recognized all the young men who worked with Señor Gonzalez. But they were not moving. In fact, they looked frozen. How odd....

"Excuse me," she said to the old man, placing her hand on his arm. "Something's going on at the helo. I'll be back in a moment. You stay here with your daughter, okay?"

"Well...but of course, Señorita Rhona...."

She saw the nonplussed look on the old gentleman's face and gave him a quick smile of reassurance. He looked worried.

"What is it? What's wrong, *señorita?*"

"I don't know," Rhona said, putting her glasses back on. "Let me go check it out, okay? Stay here...."

Her heartbeat quickened. Something *was* wrong. No one was moving. She couldn't see Nolan. The only people visible from this vantage point were the young men. Their arms were tense at their sides as they all looked toward the Huey. Fear bolted through Rhona. Her mind spun with possibilities. Had one of the people of the barrio argued with Nolan? Was there a disagreement with someone she couldn't see?

Hurrying her steps, Rhona automatically took stock

of everyone's position. Her old combat instincts took over. She was scared, but she was thinking through the rush of adrenaline now pumping hard through her system. What was wrong?

The young men were tall, all of them six feet or more. They had formed a semicircle around the opening to the fuselage of the Huey. The flatbed truck was only a few feet away. Unholstering her .45 from where it hung on the front of her flak vest, Rhona decided to play it safe. She was going to assume that someone was at risk. It had to be Nolan, who was still out of sight.

Her heart pounded furiously with dread. Lifting the pistol up near her body, she kept her footsteps light and soundless. Luckily, she was five foot nine inches tall, so the young men provided cover for her approach. Still, Rhona was wary. Heading toward the front of the truck, she moved up against the right fender. Keying her hearing, she tried to listen over the pounding of her heart.

A voice. A man's voice. Threatening. Gulping, Rhona realized it wasn't a voice she recognized. Bending down, she inched forward to the end of the truck to try and hear who was speaking. Crouching down, she took off the safety on her pistol and locked and loaded it. A bullet was now in the chamber.

What she heard next sent a chill straight to her pounding heart.

"I told you, Mr. Pilot, to call your copilot back here now or I'm gonna blow a hole through that head of yours. You got that?"

Nolan was sure his temple was being bruised by the point of the Beretta 9 mm pistol barrel, which was being jammed repeatedly into his head. The man was short—only five-foot-ten—but he had his hand, like an eagle's claw, on Nolan's left shoulder, the gun at his head. Nolan faced the Huey, his heart in chaos. The man, who called himself Frank, was a member of Diablo. He'd caught Nolan from behind at the door of the helo. And he'd told everyone to freeze or he'd blow Nolan's head off. No one moved.

Sweat ran down Nolan's face. Out of the corner of his eye, he could see Frank, grinning at him triumphantly. The man, who was probably in his thirties, had a scraggly brown beard and smelled like he desperately needed a bath. The look in his blue, ferretlike eyes was dangerous. Nolan had seen the same glitter in the gaze of a wild animal when it caught its quarry.

"I told you, I don't know where she is," he rasped, his voice low and taut.

"Lyin' bastard," Frank hissed. Again he jammed the gun into Nolan's temple. "Call her back here *now*, fly boy, or you're dead meat just like those two pilots we capped the other day."

Rage flowed through Nolan. "You...murdered them...." The words came out strangled, with barely held rage.

Laughing harshly, Frank said, "Yeah, fly boy. They didn't know what was comin'. They thought we were Goody Two-shoes like these idiots surroundin' us! Now, call the slut, will you? I'm short on patience and

I got an itchy trigger finger, besides. Wanna test me on it? Huh? Go ahead, try me.''

Nolan's hands slowly closed into fists as his mind churned with possibilities on how he could disarm the son of a bitch. No way would he call Rhona over here. No, this bastard had already killed his two friends. Nolan was damned if Rhona was going to become a target. Somehow, some way, he had to get the upper hand on this gloating lunatic.

As Nolan stood there, wavering, with Frank's fetid breath making him nauseous, he felt the man's hand tighten on his uniform. He saw the man's finger brush the trigger. Tense, his eyes darting around him, Frank lifted his lips to reveal his yellow, coated teeth.

"Dammit, I said *call her.* Do it *now* or I'm gonna drop you and go find her myself!''

Sucking in a breath of air, Nolan steeled himself. There was no way in hell he was going to give up Rhona to this wild-eyed, crazy bastard. The guy was hopped-up on something, more than likely cocaine, because he couldn't stand still. He was aggressive, eyes darting, always jerking and moving. The only thing he kept steady was the gun barrel against Nolan's aching, bruised temple.

"Go to hell,'' Nolan muttered between gritted teeth. In those seconds, as he saw the man's finger again brush the trigger, Nolan realized that he loved Rhona. Love. Real, honest-to-God love. The kind he wanted again, but had despaired of ever finding after his wife's untimely death. And now he would never get to tell Rhona that. She would never know. One kiss.

They'd shared one kiss that had made their worlds stand still, melt together and become one. Why had he been so blind? Why hadn't he realized when he'd shared that deep, tender, searching kiss with her that he loved her?

His life began flashing before his eyes, from the time he was a young child onward. Nolan closed his eyes and waited. He stopped breathing. This was the end. He didn't want to die. He wanted to live—live to tell Rhona he loved her, and wanted to share his life with her if she'd have him—but none of those things were going to happen now. Because, in a few seconds, he was going to be dead, his brains splattered across the fuselage of the Huey. What a hell of a way to go....

Nine

January 11: 1110

Just as Nolan drew in what he believed would be his last breath of air, he heard a commotion off to his left. Slanting a glance in that direction, he saw the young men part like the Red Sea. Then Rhona stood there. His eyes widened. Somehow she had slid soundlessly between the Latinos, her gun drawn and raised. The look in her slitted eyes was one of rage. Her mouth was grim. Her hands were held out in front of her, wrapped around the .45—which was aimed at Frank.

And then, to his horror, Nolan heard Frank curse. The man jerked the pistol away from his temple and in one single, smooth motion, aimed it directly at Rhona. *No! Oh, God! No!*

Breathing hard, Rhona saw the gunman turn his aim away from Nolan and toward her, fury and surprise erupting in his narrowed eyes.

There was no time to think; only to react. Rhona's finger brushed the trigger, but before she could get a shot off, she saw the barrel of her opponent's gun explode with a red-and-yellow flash.

The bullet hit her high, near her left collarbone. She grunted, thrown backward by the force of the blast.

Nolan reacted swiftly, whirling toward the gunman with his fists clenched and delivering two solid blows to his chest. At the same time, the gunman got off two more shots.

The second and third rounds struck her low, in the abdomen, sending Rhona flying off her feet. But not before she fired back, the barrel leveled at the gunman's head.

A cry ripped from Nolan's mouth as he saw Rhona go down. Her uniform fabric exploded. Bits and pieces of cloth fragments flew into the air like confetti suddenly released. At the same time, the rupture of gunfire shattered his eardrums, and Nolan heard Frank grunt as the pistol fell from his nerveless fingers and he crumpled backward.

Then the air was filled with shouts and cries as terror reigned. But Nolan's only concern right now was for Rhona, and he raced to her side.

No! God no! Not her! Don't let her die!

The Latinos stood back, their mouths agape, their eyes wide with confusion and terror. As Nolan dropped to his knees beside Rhona he felt tears jam into his eyes. She lay on her back, unconscious.

He reached out with unsteady hands to touch her hair, which had come loose in a tangled mass. Her eyes were closed and she lay like a puppet, sprawled out on the yellow dirt. Calling her name, he leaned over her.

"Rhona! Rhona! Can you hear me? Wake up!" Nolan shouted, staring in shock at the three bullet holes in the fabric of her flight suit. Gripping her gently by the shoulders, he leaned closer.

"Do you hear me? God, say you can hear me! Rhona?" His voice broke with terror. Running his badly shaking hand across her limp body, he tried to find the wound so he could staunch the flow of blood he was sure was pumping from her limp body.

And then he remembered that she was wearing a flak vest beneath her one-piece flight suit. With trembling hands, he ripped open the Velcro that held her uniform together from throat to crotch. As the suit was peeled away, he saw Rhona's dark green Kevlar vest beneath it. Sobbing, Nolan tried to steady himself. He loved Rhona. She couldn't be dead! She just couldn't! And yet she'd taken three direct hits, at close range.

Peeling the upper part of her flight suit wider, he gasped. There were three deep indentations in Rhona's Kevlar vest. Had the bullets penetrated it, and was she bleeding out beneath it? Nolan's hands would barely work as he fumbled with the Velcro openings located at her right shoulder and along her rib cage. Pulling the vest open, he frantically searched her smooth, golden flesh beneath her white cotton chemise. Three ugly black-and-blue bruises were already forming, swelling up in huge welts.

His breath came out ragged with relief. None of the bullets had penetrated the vest. It had saved her life.

He didn't know what to do first—cry or hold Rhona. As he took off the vest and handed it to one of the Latino teens, who had knelt down opposite him to help, more tears flooded Nolan's eyes.

Rhona groaned softly.

Once Nolan had closed the front of her flight suit, he lifted his head toward hers. Her black lashes fluttered faintly. Anxiety shot through him.

"He's dead," one of the teens said. He was kneeling over Frank, his fingers on the carotid artery of the gunman's neck.

"Good," Nolan snarled. "Get his pistol. And stay alert. There could be more of the Diablo gang around."

Worried murmurs rippled through the group. They quickly formed a protective circle around Nolan and Rhona.

All his focus, all his life energy was trained on Rhona as her lashes lifted. Her eyes were confused and turgid-looking, he noted. When she lifted her hand weakly, he caught it and held it tightly in his.

"You're okay, Rhona, you're okay...." he breathed. Leaning over, he ran his trembling hand across her head which was covered with dust and bits of grass.

Nolan's voice penetrated Rhona's consciousness.

When she opened her eyes and saw his frantic expression—the terror banked in his narrowed green gaze—she wondered if she was dead. Bits and pieces of the gun battle drifted back to her. As Nolan caught her hand, and she felt its warm pressure, sure and steadying, she decided she wasn't dead after all. The last thing she remembered was the savage look on Frank's face as he'd pulled the trigger to kill her.

"N-Nolan?" Her voice was wobbly. "You're okay?"

He laughed unsteadily. "Me, darlin'? I'm *fine*. Fine! It's you I was worried about." Leaning down, he pressed a kiss to her furrowed forehead. "You're okay, Rhona. The vest stopped the bullets. You aren't dying, thank God. You've got three hellacious bruises where the bullets hit your vest, but you're going to be okay—" He choked up abruptly.

Nolan couldn't stop caressing her head. He needed to touch her. The love spilling through him right now was like a river, like a mountain cataract, powerful and unrestrained. Cupping her chin, he leaned very close so she could hear him. Speaking in a low tone, enunciating every word clearly so that she would understand him, he told her, "Just lie still. Get your bearings. I love you, Rhona. Just know that. Hang on to that. I'm here. I'll protect you…."

His words flowed like balm over her shattered emotions. Rhona clung to his gaze, the words sinking into her consciousness, calming her pounding heart. She felt as if her body was one huge ache, throbbing with fire where the bullets had struck her vest. But she was going to live! The tears in Nolan's eyes convinced her that was real. She wasn't dead, she was alive! And Nolan was here at her side, leaning over her. His mouth was contorted, and he seemed close to tears. The way he gripped her hand was almost painful, but that felt good to her because it reassured her she wasn't dead, but alive.

"The gunman?" she croaked.

Nolan briefly lifted his head and looked over his shoulder. "Dead."

"Oh, no…." Rhona closed her eyes again. Pain and regret assailed her, like razors slashing into her heart.

"Oh, no?" Nolan snorted violently. He released her hand and pulled her into his arms. Rhona sighed and rested her head against his shoulder, eyes closed. "You killed him out of self-defense," Nolan whispered raggedly, holding her tightly against him. He looked up. Señor Gonzalez was approaching, terror clearly visible in his pale features. One of the young men rushed to his side and told him that Rhona was all right. Instantly the elder's face was flooded with relief.

All his assistants were spooked, however, and looked around nervously. Nolan didn't feel safe, either. Where there was one Diablo gang member, there were probably more. He gathered Rhona against him, pressed a kiss to her smudged, pale cheek and whispered. "Come on, try to stand. I need to get you out of here and to the base hospital. You need medical help. Can you stand up?"

Everything seemed to be shorting out around

Rhona. She'd been in combat before, so she recognized the symptoms. Her only contact with reality right now was the feel of Nolan's arms around her. Gripping his hand, she nodded and pushed herself upward. With his help, she stood. Immediately she felt flashes of severe pain, and she groaned and pressed her hand against her abdomen. Nausea followed.

"I think I'm gonna heave," she whispered.

Nolan nodded. "That's okay," he breathed raggedly. "That's okay, darlin'. Do what you have to do...."

Just seeing the gunman's unmoving body made her gag. Rhona felt as if she were in an ongoing nightmare. Her knees buckling, she leaned down and vomited. Nolan held her by the shoulders, his body a bulwark to lean against as she heaved out the terror that clawed violently in her belly. Tears streaked through the dirt on her face.

Someone, a young Latino, pushed toward her a damp piece of cloth he'd torn from his T-shirt, so she could wipe her mouth and runny nose afterward. She was touched by his thoughtfulness and kindness. The care made Rhona cry. Every face around her was filled with such concern for her.

Rhona didn't feel right. She hadn't sustained a bullet wound, but felt gut-punched. Pain was ripping up and down from her abdomen to her collarbone. Somehow, Nolan helped her clean up, and someone handed her a bottle of water so she could rinse out her mouth.

Many hands helped to lift her from her kneeling position and walk her gently to the Huey. En route,

Rhona turned her head, unable to look at her attacker. She'd taken a life, and that shattered her in another way. This was different than the Gulf War. Or was it? Her emotions were shredded.

As Nolan eased her into the copilot's seat and strapped her in, all she could do was sit there and stare ahead like a zombie. Rhona felt torn apart, as if she were in a bad movie where everything happened in slow motion. The sensation was familiar, for she'd felt it as she'd held Jake in her arms while he bled to death beside the crashed helicopter.

Nolan got Consuelo strapped into the back seat for the ride to the hospital. She was very pale and holding her swollen belly. The gunfight must have rattled her deeply.

After sliding the door shut and locking it, Nolan squeezed between the seats.

He patted Rhona's drooping shoulder gently. "We're going home, darlin'. Just hang on, okay?"

Rhona looked in his direction. Everything was still happening in slow motion. She knew it was shock. Nolan's voice sounded as if it was coming from a tunnel, as if he was far, far away from her.

The sound of the door shutting, the hum of the engine revving, and the sight of Nolan's hands flying across the cockpit panel to get the bird operational were oddly soothing to Rhona. She was alive. Nolan was alive. They'd survived.

Closing her eyes, Rhona tipped her head back against the seat rest. The main thought throbbing through her heart and brain was the memory that No-

lan had said he loved her. Even more powerful was
the raw, naked feeling that told her she loved him, too,
with a fierceness that defied description.

January 11: 1500

"How are you feeling?" Nolan asked, as he came
to stand next to the bed where Rhona lay. She was in
a hospital room with four other patients, so he kept
his voice low. When he'd walked in, still dressed in
his flight suit, she'd appeared to be sleeping. But as
he approached, she opened her eyes and looked toward
the door where he stood, as she sensed his presence.
Nolan saw that the other three patients in the room,
all civilians, were in a lot worse shape than Rhona
was. Still, they watched Nolan and Rhona together
with varying degrees of interest. They had nothing better to do, Nolan realized.

Smiling tenderly down at Rhona, he reached out and
caught her hand as she lifted it toward him. Dressed
in a pale blue cotton gown, she looked drained, her
recently washed black hair framing her drawn features.
When he slid his fingers around hers, her hand felt
damp and cool.

"I'm okay...." Rhona whispered.

"Liar."

One corner of her mouth lifted. "Can't fool you,
can I?"

"Why would you want to, darlin'?" He saw her
lashes close. They were beaded with tears. "I just
talked to the doc, and she said you're going to feel

beat-up, black-and-blue, for a good two weeks after this little incident.''

Nodding, Rhona swallowed hard, opened her eyes and looked at Nolan as he rested an arm on the stainless steel bar that bordered her bed. His other hand squeezed hers, as that charming Irish smile settled on his strong male mouth.

"Yes, I know," Rhona replied. "The doctor just left about ten minutes ago. Did you see Morgan? Laura?"

"Yeah, that's where I just came from. They're upset, but relieved to hear you're still around. Morgan is going to drop by and see you as soon as he can, but he's in a meeting right now." Lifting her hand, Nolan kissed the back of it gently, his mouth lingering.

A sigh rippled from her. "I was never so scared, Nolan. I—well, I wasn't sure *what* to do. The teenagers were a wall around you. I couldn't just come in with gun blazing. I didn't want to hurt them."

"Listen, darlin', you did a helluva good job in a situation even a Recon Marine would double up over. There was no target opportunity. You did the exact right thing."

"I was so scared he was going to kill you...." She gave a sob, then got hold of her emotions.

Leaning over, Nolan brushed a tear from her cheekbone. "My life was passin' before my eyes, Rhona. I knew I was going to die."

"You refused to tell him where I was."

Continuing to gently stroke her damp cheek with his fingertips, he said in a raspy tone, "There's not a chance I'd ever have told that bastard where you were. I knew he meant business. He'd have killed both of us, Rhona. Just like he did my two friends...and..." Nolan shut his eyes for a moment, wrestling with his emotions. Opening them, he whispered, "No way was I going to put you into the line of fire."

"You were giving your life for me."

Shrugging, he tried to buck her up. "You're worth a helluva lot more than the likes of me, darlin'. Of course I'd give my life for you." More tears were leaking from the corners of her eyes. The doctor had warned him that Rhona would cycle up and down emotionally for a number of days, as she got over the shock of nearly dying. Because of this, the doctor had urged Nolan to be a witness, a set of ears, a shoulder to cry on if that's what Rhona needed, in order to heal herself after her ordeal. That was an easy prescription for him to fill. He loved her, so it wasn't a duty, it was a blessing in disguise.

With her other hand, she shakily tried to wipe the tears from her eyes. "You were worth saving, Nolan Galway."

Giving her a look of pride, he whispered, "You're one courageous woman, Rhona. I wasn't looking for rescue. All I wanted was for you to escape that bastard. I wanted you to live...."

Sniffing, Rhona said, "Help me sit up? My gut feels like it's been beat with baseball bats."

Placing his arm behind her shoulders, Nolan helped to reposition her. Stuffing several pillows behind her back, he fluffed them up until he was satisfied she was comfortable.

Dragging her fingers through her hair, Rhona held his lingering green gaze. "I don't want to stay here, Nolan. The doctor said she was giving me a sick chit for seven days. She said I had a room reserved over at the B.O.Q. Could you bring my clothes from our tent? My flight uniform is literally shot to hell and I can't wear it. They cut it off me in the emergency room."

"Yeah." He chuckled. "I saw. Sure, I'll bring your civilian clothes over."

"I don't like hospitals. Besides, I'm not hurt. They can use this bed for someone who really needs it." Not only that, the smell of antiseptic was strong, and it always turned Rhona's stomach.

Patting her shoulder, he said, "No problem. I understand."

"What about you, Nolan? What's going to happen now that they've taken me off flight duty for a week? Have the replacement pilots come in yet? Are you still flying or did they put you on flight waivers, too?"

"Nah, I can fly, as long as they can get me a replacement copilot. They gave me forty-eight hours, though." His eyes gleamed. "They authorized me a room at the B.O.Q., too." His mouth curved faintly. "Think we can share a room instead? I don't know about you, but tonight I'd like to share a nice, soft bed with the woman I've fallen in love with. I have a lot I want to share with her, tell her. What do you think, darlin'?"

Sniffing, Rhona gave him a warm, helpless look. "You're so brazen, Galway."

"Upon occasion. Especially once I've made up my mind about something."

Not wanting to talk of their personal lives where Rhona was sure three other patients were listening, she reached out and grazed his unshaved chin. "Yes, let's share a room. Can you take care of the details?"

"After you saving my no-good arse, I think I can handle something simple like that for us," he teased. Leaning over, he placed a chaste, warm kiss on her temple. "Just rest, Rhona. I'll be back sooner than you think…."

She sat there, her legs crossed beneath the light blue coverlet, her hands in her lap. Emotionally, Rhona felt like she was on a roller coaster. Gently touching her deeply bruised, swollen abdomen, she grimaced. Nolan's certainty about his love for her was scary. And wonderful. Frowning, she reached for the glass of water on the bedstand nearby. Just having the ability to drink a glass of water when she needed it wasn't wasted on her. No, out there in the basin, people were slowly dehydrating to the point that they would begin to die because there wasn't enough water. Luckily, Camp Reed had a series of wells. The earthquake hadn't shattered them, so they were in good working order. Everyone on the military base had all the water they wanted.

Looking toward the door, Rhona felt herself pining for Nolan. How could he have taken root in her heart so soon? She was mystified and stunned by it all. She ached to be in his arms, just to be held, because right now, in the aftermath of that horrible shoot-out, she felt like a scared little girl. Worse, she had taken another human's life. Oh, it was true she'd been in the navy, but she'd flown troop and cargo helicopters that weren't armed. She was willing to give her life for her country, but the thought of taking another human's life hadn't been a part of her reality. And now it had happened.

Pressing her hands to her face, she found her shoulders shaking as she cried silently. She cried for the family of the gunman, whose name, she'd learned, was Frank. Just because he was bad didn't mean a mother wasn't going to miss her son, or sisters wouldn't miss their brother. Or a father wouldn't grieve. Life was precious. And all around them, life and death were entwined, the wall between almost transparent in the aftermath of the quake. She knew, more than ever, that every moment, every hour, was precious and should be lived to the utmost.

She had just found love in the most unexpected place, at the most unexpected time. Nolan, who had been her enemy, was now her lover…or soon to be. Rhona could not deny the love she felt for him. It had engulfed her like a volcanic eruption as she realized his life was being threatened. Something primeval, surprising and powerful had overwhelmed her fear and anxiety as she'd risked her own life to save his. That's what people in love did: they took care of one another through thick and thin, in good and bad circumstances. Yes, she loved him. But what did it all mean? Rhona wanted nothing more than to be in a quiet room, alone, with Nolan. They had so much to talk about, to share…to show one another with loving touches. So much, in a world gone insane.

Ten

January 18: 0030

"It's our last night together here. We'd better enjoy it," Rhona murmured as she lifted the covers to share the bed with Nolan.

Nolan felt Rhona slide into the soft, large bed and snuggle up to him, her naked form against his. How easy it was to slip his arm beneath her neck and shoulder and bring her into the circle of his embrace.

"No need to convince me," he said, laughing softly as he pressed several small kisses to her freshly washed hair.

"Seven days of enforced sick leave and I'm going bats," Rhona muttered, as she closed her eyes and relaxed against his hard, warm body. It was midnight, and Nolan had just finished the last of his duties at Ops before coming over to the B.O.Q. to share the room with her.

Chuckling, Nolan moved his hand with fond familiarity across her strong, lean back. "Well, come 0500 tomorrow, you're going to be my copilot again, and you, too, can put in twelve-hour days." He felt her purr with satisfaction. Already, his body was hardening with need of her, as always. Because of her injuries, they'd agreed not to try and love one another the past six days. Rhona had been too sore and bruised to do much of anything at first. She'd had hot baths, used ice packs on her bruised flesh and slept a lot to catch up on what she lost to nightmares each night. She'd even begun to lend a willing hand at the hospital during the day. She couldn't just stay in this room and do nothing. While Nolan flew today, she'd worked with Laura Trayhern and helped feed the babies in the nursery, which overflowed with new arrivals.

"Mmm, I can hardly wait. I'm bored to death around here," she murmured, pressing a kiss to the side of his recently shaved jaw. Sharing a shower with Nolan had been an incredibly heated experience. Rhona ached to love him fully, to claim him and share with him. Tonight was the night.

For Nolan, it had been six of the most exquisite, torturous days of his life. But it had also been enriching in so many ways. Because although he could not share sexual gratification with Rhona, every night he looked forward to the precious hours he'd spend with her in his arms. They would talk of the day's events.

More importantly, Nolan knew, he'd listen as Rhona talked, divesting herself of the guilt, anger, depression and anxieties that grew out of the shooting of the Diablo gang member.

There was a special satisfaction in talking deep into the night, with her wrapped in his arms. The warm, exploratory kisses, the touches meant to caress and heal her, were ways that Nolan could tell her he loved her. No, this past week had been hell on earth for him, physically speaking, but the time had given them the rare gifts of being able to explore and learn more about one another. To become friends before they became lovers.

Rhona looked at Nolan's profile above her. The lights outside the B.O.Q. filtered in through the closed drapes, giving just enough of a glow to see his strong, rakish face.

"You're smiling, Nolan Galway," she whispered wickedly, sliding her fingertips across his curved lower lip. How much she enjoyed kissing that mouth, and tonight, the hunger for him she'd felt so strongly, for so long, would be satiated.

"Wouldn't you be?" he whispered back, even more wickedly. Gently turning her onto her back, Nolan rested on his side above her. Rhona wore no clothing to bed; she hadn't from the beginning, because the nightgown always tangled irritably between her legs and would wake her up at night. Nolan liked that because he never wore anything to bed, either. Watching the play of shadows across her face, her gray eyes warm with desire for him, he lifted his hand and cupped her chin.

"Yes." She laughed softly. "I'm hungry, sweetheart…and not for food. For you…"

"Music to my ears." He sighed, gliding his fingertips down her neck. Avoiding the still swollen and bruised flesh that was healing near her left collarbone, he lightly grazed her left breast.

A ragged sigh issued from her parting lips. Drowning in his lambent green gaze, Rhona said, "I want to love you, Nolan…. Don't treat me like fragile china, okay? I'm bruised and sore, but I'm tired of waiting. I want you…."

"I'm beginning to really like women warriors," he murmured, placing his lips against her brow, then her cheek, and finally, her lips. "They are bold, brazen and fearless when it comes to telling a man what they want."

Laughter bubbled up from her throat as she gloried in the brush of his strong, cherishing mouth against hers. "I'm only brazen, bold and fearless with *you*. I'm not like this ordinarily," she said, sliding her hand across his hip and down his strong thigh.

As he pressed his mouth to hers, Nolan felt her lips open like a blossom and welcome him eagerly. The last week spent exploring, talking and sharing was making this night with Rhona, their physical coupling, so very special.

"I need you," he told her, looking down into her half-closed eyes. "And I love you, Rhona. With my heart…my soul…"

His words vibrated through her like thunder rolling across the vales and swales of her beloved desert. Breath hitching as his fingers followed the curve of her breast, she arched toward him.

"You are my moonbow," she whispered as she moved her hand in a warm, exploratory fashion down the taut, warm length of his belly. "A rainbow around the moon in a dark night sky," she murmured against his mouth. "You give color, meaning, richness to me, Nolan…and I love you so much it hurts…."

Lifting his head, Nolan smiled tenderly down at her and caressed her loose, damp hair. "One of the many things I've come to appreciate about you is how you see the natural world, and how we're all a part of it."

"Like me seeing you as my moonbow?"

Nodding, Nolan grazed her flushed cheek and absorbed the silver sparkle in her drowsy, luminous eyes. Her lips were parted, moist and beckoning to him. "Yeah, I hope I can always bring color, laughter, hope and happiness into your life, darlin'. You certainly bring that into mine…." And he leaned down and captured the hardened peak of her breast. Instantly, she moaned, pressing her lower body demandingly against his. The time for talk was over, like a shimmering rainbow moving on with a passing shower.

The heat in her aching lower body exploded. Moaning his name over and over, her hands opening and closing frantically against his taut, damp shoulders as he moved above her, Rhona could do little but let all the emotions she felt toward him flood her. Yes, he was a moonbow, a man who had come to her as dark and threatening as the night. Yet like the moon, whose luminescence exposed the darkness, Nolan had owned up to his unhealthy prejudice toward women. He had transformed a negative, a darkness, into something positive and beautiful—something that included Rhona, showed her respect and even admiration.

As his knee moved between her legs, she opened to him, welcoming him, urging him to come into her, to complete the rainbow of colors she ached to share with him. As his hands framed her face, she opened her eyes and looked up at him. Nolan's eyes were narrowed and intense, his face a mask of taut desire barely leashed. Excitement throbbed through her as she parted her thighs so that he could surge forward into her.

Lifting her hands, Rhona ran them across his bunched, tense shoulders. His lips lifted away from his clenched teeth. She felt the power, the thrust as he slid into her hot, moist depths. Her moan joined his as they surged together like the ocean crashing onto golden, sandy shores. And shutting her eyes again, she actually saw the scintillating colors of the moonbow at night, red-violet meeting and melding with a shimmering cobalt-blue, and the palest of lilac turning soft fuchsia, then pink....

Rhona welcomed him fully into her. Joy overwhelmed her as he moved with her like the tides of the great ocean, gliding together with a oneness that made her gasp in delight.

The feel of Nolan's breath, warm and moist against her mouth as they clung to one another, only heightened the boiling need that was moving toward an explosion within Rhona. His hands were strong, cherishing and caressing, urging her to participate wildly in their meeting and mating.

As he suckled her, slid his hand beneath her hip and brought her tightly against him, her world collided with his. A bolt of wild, frantic lightning exploded deep within her, and she cried out with exquisite pleasure and surprise. Almost simultaneously, she felt Nolan drag in a breath, and then a primal growl rolled through him, vibrating through her in turn as he spilled himself deep within her singing, shuddering form.

Once again colored lights shimmered brightly behind her closed eyes. Rhona felt his mouth, rough and demanding, against hers. Meeting and matching his frantic, pleasurable kiss, which made her soar on the arc of the rainbow about the moon, she became one with him.

A long time later, it was over. She felt Nolan's hard length and weight move off her. When he lay at her side, he drew her tightly against him, kissing her eyes, cheek and mouth repeatedly. As he caressed her hair, she sighed, relishing the minor explosions, the heat and pleasure, still bubbling within her.

Nolan felt Rhona's arms, strong and nurturing, move around his neck. Just the soft brush of her lips against his cheek, his mouth and neck, sent his heart soaring. The fierceness with which he loved her left him stunned and shaken. Slowly, he became aware once more of their surroundings. The weak light peeking through the drawn curtains illuminated her soft, satisfied expression as he gazed at her.

"I love you," he told her, his voice unsteady, his hand cupping her flushed cheek. "I don't know when it happened, Rhona, or how or why. And I don't care…."

Nodding, her throat closing with sudden, unexpected tears, she realized Nolan was completely vulnerable to her. He was able to share his heart, his feelings with her, and that elated her as little else ever could. "I know…I feel the same, sweetheart."

"I know it's too soon," he told her, his voice husky, "but I like what we have. We got off to a rocky start, thanks to me," he said, his voice wry with mild derision.

She saw his mouth hitch upward in sincere apology. Reaching over, she stroked her fingers against his damp brow and nudged back several strands of dark hair. "Nolan, you were wrong and you admitted it. That's one of many things I've come to like and love about you. We're not always going to do everything right. We'll make a lot of mistakes, but the key here is getting pride and stubbornness out of the way and admitting when we're wrong." Rhona's mouth curved wickedly. "Besides, I like the making up that happens afterward."

Chuckling, he combed his fingers through the silky, ebony strands of her hair. "No argument from me. I think I'll try to be wrong a *lot*."

"You're such a ham!" Rhona laughed delightedly. "Have you thought about the fact that as of tomorrow night we are going to be sleeping on the hard, cold ground in our sleeping bags?''

His brows rose, and he chuckled. "So? We'll just zip them together and make a nice, cozy bed for both of us." Tracing a finger across her smiling mouth, he whispered, "Besides, I don't think we'll feel the hard ground beneath us. If our lovemaking out there is half of what we shared just now, I won't feel the ground, I'll just feel you."

His compliment warmed her heart. She smiled and then became more serious. "We need to talk about the future, Nolan. I wasn't planning on falling in love with a marine pilot, believe me."

Seeing her seriousness, the worry in her eyes, Nolan stopped smiling. Then he laid his hand against her naked shoulder and caressed it gently. "Listen to me, darlin'. We have *time*."

"In one way, we do, Nolan, but in another... Well, that day that Frank was going to kill you brought home to me the need to live every minute of my life in the *now*. Not as some future thing waiting to happen."

Bringing her into his arms, he drew the sheet up over them. This was a discussion he'd known was coming and he hoped he had the right words for what he had to say. As Rhona pressed her face against his jaw and neck, he murmured, "Standing there with that gun pressed against my temple, I didn't think I was going to live, either." Nolan's voice was deep and troubled. "The only thing I regretted, Rhona, was that I hadn't told you I loved you. Standing there, I realized I did love you. And in the next second, I felt a sadness like I've never felt in my life—that I hadn't had a chance to tell you. What I didn't say. Well, that taught me a helluva good lesson—to share with you what's in my heart and head in the moment—because there might not be another one coming.''

"Awful way to learn it—with a gun to your head, literally," Rhona murmured worriedly.

Sighing, Nolan said, "Yes, but it brought home to me what you'd said earlier about men being closed up like clams and not sharing their thoughts and feelings with the women they love. I understand that now as never before."

"I like hearing you think out loud, Nolan. About how you're feeling. It helps me stop guessing about how you're really feeling versus what I think you're feeling. It stops a lot of possible misunderstandings and assumptions before they get started."

"I see that now, too," he murmured, smiling down at her. Rhona looked incredibly beautiful in that moment, her hair in soft disarray around her face, her eyes slumberous, and that sensual mouth of hers soft and well kissed. "Friends talk to one another. We're learning how to talk and share with one another, darlin'. I like it. I want it to continue."

Heart singing, she whispered, "So do I. I like you being my friend...and my lover. It's a great combination."

"So, where do we go from here?"

"We'll have weeks...months...of flying together," Rhona said.

"Yeah, I like that part of it. We just need to keep our relationship behind closed tent flaps."

Rhona agreed. The military would frown upon their having a personal relationship with one another. Only at night, behind the closed flaps of their small tent, could they be intimate. "I can handle it, Nolan. Can you?"

"Barely."

She laughed softly.

"You're so beautiful," he told her. "It's going to be hell keeping my hands off you in the cockpit, stopping myself from reaching out to touch you like this...." And he trailed his fingers across her soft cheek.

Closing her eyes, Rhona sighed raggedly. "I know what you mean. It won't be easy for me to keep my hands off you, either. I'm a toucher...."

"Yeah, I like the way you touch me." Nolan smiled into her opening eyes.

"I'm even more worried about the Diablo gang, Nolan. You found out from Morgan three days after the shooting that Frank wasn't working alone, but that the rest of the gang are still in area five. They must miss Frank by now. They must know something happened to him."

Hearing the fear and concern in her voice, Nolan leaned down and kissed her lips, then rasped, "We'll stay on guard, Rhona. Since that incident, Señor Gonzalez has alerted his people to be on the lookout for strangers coming into the barrio. That was the mistake we made. Everyone saw Frank nosing around, but no one stopped him, challenged him or did anything. Now we know better.'' His brow furrowed. ''And they've got the marine fire team in place in area six. The new SOP will be that when we land, they'll be there, M-16s locked and loaded. The guys and gals in Logistics know they have to protect these helicopter flights ferrying supplies to the civilians that need them.''

''Yes, but that'll limit the marines from doing much law enforcement, not to mention setting up shelters and essential services. They'll have to hang around the baseball field during daylight hours yet they have two square miles they're responsible for, filled with people who need protection from roving gangs like Diablo.'' Frustration ate at Rhona. ''They won't be able to keep the whole area protected, Nolan, if they're meeting us every time we land.''

''Shh,'' he whispered, pressing his finger to her lips. ''Listen, darlin', we can't solve the world's problems tonight. This earthquake disaster is stretching us in ways none of us could ever have envisioned. We had all hoped that no matter how desperate things got, people wouldn't resort to doing the kind of things that Diablo are doing. Even the best government emergency measures can only go so far. For experts to be able to guess what every single human in a bad situation will do to survive…well, that's impossible.''

Frustrated, Rhona whispered, ''I know you're right. I just worry about it all….''

Kissing her gently, Nolan realized where her worry was coming from. She'd had to kill a man to save a life. She had met this disaster head-on, and had to do something no one ever wanted to do: take another life. Even though they were in the military, and their careers were about protecting their country, no one wanted to take life unless absolutely necessary.

"Morgan Trayhern is working with Logistics to get more plans in place to protect the innocent people at risk in these areas. I know he's working on a new scheme of putting a Marine Recon team with a medical person into area one, which is just outside Camp Reed. The Recon team is composed of five men, one of whom is a paramedic. They can provide law enforcement plus medical expertise to the people there."

"It sounds promising, but you have only so many Recon teams in the Corps."

"I know," Nolan soothed. "We have limited trained resources, but I know Morgan is good at utilizing them in the best way possible. He's the right man for this job. He's got the vision, and he's used to working in tight, dangerous situations. He's trying to make it as safe as possible out there for us. He knows that we're the only lifeline these people have."

Closing her eyes, Rhona slid her arm around his torso. "I love you, Nolan Galway. And one day, this disaster will end."

"And when it does, what will you do?"

She smiled softly. "Go back to my eco-friendly crop-dusting business. Do what I did before. The guy I love is only twenty miles away. I think I'll keep him, and what we have."

Chuckling, Nolan said, "Yeah, I was thinking along

the same lines. When this is all over, I have a beautiful woman in my backyard to share a home with...."

Opening her eyes, Rhona gazed up into his shadowed face, which was tender with love for her. "Maybe, when this is all over, six months down the road or so, we'll want to make what we have more permanent?"

"Count on it, darlin'. You're the first woman I've loved since Carol died. What I've found with you, I want to continue to explore. This isn't some roll in the hay for me. And it's not some convenient relationship I'll throw away later."

Rhona already knew that about Nolan. He was someone she could trust with her heart, with her soul. "Same here," she told him, her voice unsteady. "But I'm going to make every day count with you, Nolan. I'm going to live every moment with you, sweetheart."

Lifting her hand, he pressed a kiss to the back of it and held her lustrous gray eyes, which were wide with love for him. "Out of the hell of a disaster, I met a woman I love more than anything. She saved my life. I want to share my life with her. Somehow, we'll get through this, together. We've got time. We've got the right stuff going for us, darlin'. And I'm planning on being with you, at your side, forever."

Epilogue

When Nolan approached their Huey the next morning, he spotted a fire team of marines waiting at parade rest nearby. With a quick glance at the helicopter, he saw Rhona was already in the cockpit, going through some preflight prep. Turning his attention back to the fire team, he saw the leader, a lance corporal dressed in combat cammies, his M-16 rifle slung across his thick, broad shoulder, give him a slight nod.

"Corporal," Nolan said, returning the salute the enlisted marine gave him as he came to attention, "you're riding with us this morning." Glancing at the set of orders in his hand, he noted the name: Lance Corporal Quinn Grayson. Looking up into the tall marine's square face, Nolan was pleased. Corporal Gray-

son and his men, who also came to attention, all
looked like seasoned vets.

"Yes, sir," Grayson replied.

"At ease," Nolan murmured, tucking the transit orders in a pocket of his flight suit. Glancing around at
the expectant marines, Nolan could see that they were
ready for combat, which was exactly what they were
going into. He and Rhona were to fly them into area
five, where they would try to stop Diablo. He wasn't
sure five men could do it, but they were marines, and
even outnumbered, they were the best trained field
force in the world, as far as he was concerned.

Besides, looking into Grayson's glacial blue eyes,
which were narrowed and thoughtful, Nolan felt a frisson of satisfaction. The leader of this fire team was no
one to mess with. That was obvious. Nolan felt sure
he had probably been in the Corps at least seven years,
and seen action in the Gulf War.

"You were briefed at Logistics on area five?" Nolan asked as the lance corporal spread his feet and
stood at ease.

"Yes, sir, we were. An hour ago."

Nodding, Nolan frowned. "It's a hot area, Corporal."

"Yes, sir, we're well aware of what this gang has
done." He smiled thinly. "And we're lookin' forward
to settlin' some scores."

Giving him a wry smile, Nolan said, "We'll be
dropping you off at a leveled shopping mall in the
center of area five. It's my understanding you'll be
meeting a policewoman by the name of Kerry Chel-

ton? She's with the Orange County Sheriff's Department, and according to my sources, knows this piece of real estate like the back of her hand. You'll be working with her.''

Scowling, Grayson said, ''Yes, sir, we've been told that she's in cell phone contact with Logistics here at the base. She's been asking for help because she can't take on Diablo by herself.''

Nolan heard the derision in the marine's deep voice. ''Just because she's a woman,'' he told the leader lightly, ''doesn't mean she can't do her job as a law enforcement officer. Right now we need every able-bodied man and woman in the basin to help us out of this mess, Corporal.'' He sensed the man's prejudice against this woman cop. Nolan laughed to himself. Hadn't he been against Rhona at first? And judging from the flash of well-disguised anger in the towering corporal's eyes, Nolan knew that Kerry Chelton would have her hands full with this marine.

''I hear you loud and clear, sir,'' Grayson said, trying to sound sincere. Privately, Quinn disregarded Chelton as nothing more than a cardboard cop whom he had to work with. She had information. That's what he and his fire team needed. What he didn't need was *her*. He knew that they were going into a hot zone where Diablo shot first and asked questions later. War-time maneuvers were no place for wimpy females who weren't as physically strong as he and his team. No, he'd meet this woman, get rid of her as quickly as possible and then go put some hurt on the Diablo. His team was more than ready to sink their collective teeth into this renegade group that was adding to the misery of the civilian population.

"Okay..." Nolan said, a warning in his voice. Looking around, he said, "Get onboard, men. Strap in. And we'll take off for area five."

"Yes, sir," Quinn said, barely disguised excitement in his tone as he lifted his hand and ordered his men into the Huey.

*   *   *   *   *

Next month, look for

THE WILL TO LOVE,

when

MORGAN'S MERCENARIES:
ULTIMATE RESCUE

*continues in the Silhouette Romance line!
Only from* USA TODAY *bestselling
author*

LINDSAY McKENNA.

Turn the page for a sneak preview....

One

For the first time since the earthquake, Kerry Chelton felt hope. Oh, it wasn't much more than a thin, fragile thread, but it began to take root in her traumatized heart and lift her flagging spirit.

Dressed in the dark green slacks and tan long-sleeved blouse that was her sheriff's deputy uniform, she stood at the ready in the massive asphalt parking lot of the destroyed shopping center as she watched the two U.S. Marine Corps helicopters landing. A sudden, unexpected joy enveloped her. She was getting help! Help! Oh, how badly she needed some.

Putting up her hands to protect her eyes from the flying debris being kicked up by the helicopters, she surveyed the group of twenty people standing around her, respectful of her authority and leadership as they waited with her for the Huey, which was bearing a badly needed supply of bottled water.

Her gaze moved to the second Huey, which she knew carried the five marines Morgan Trayhern had sent. Morgan had been her life line since she'd cobbled the generator and radio together. His deep, soothing voice over the radio day after day had given her hope and kept her sanity. Now he had sent her reinforcements to help keep area five stable. Morgan had spoken enthusiastically of the leader of the fire team, Corporal Quinn Grayson, who was a marine as well as an EMT. God knew, area five needed medical intervention as well. She could hardly wait to meet him.

Deep within her, Kerry knew she was still in pulverizing shock over the past events. She had felt nothing, emotionally, for two weeks. Now, a trickle of hope wound through her hard-beating heart as the Huey with the marines landed within two hundred feet of her. The wind buffeting her, Kerry spread her feet apart in order to remain standing. As the Huey powered down, she saw the door slide open.

The first Marine off loading had to be Quinn Grayson, Kerry thought. She could tell by the sense of authority in his stance that he was the leader. He was six feet tall, in uniform and carrying an M-16 in his hands as he warily looked around. Turning, he spoke an order, and four more Marines disembarked, attentive, on guard and alert.

Instantly, Kerry liked Grayson. She could tell by the way his gaze searched the knot of people where she stood that he was looking for her. As she stepped out of the crowd, she saw him halt and stare hard at her. It was an assessing look: he was clearly trying to figure out if she was a friend or an enemy. Her heart fluttered wildly in her chest for a moment. That was an odd reaction, she thought as she walked quickly toward him.

She hadn't smiled in two weeks, but she did now. A smile of welcome, but also of relief. Although she could usually carry a heavy load, this disaster had stressed her out completely. And Grayson looked strong, capable and powerful as he stood there looking at her through his narrowed blue eyes. Kerry felt his gaze move over her as she closed the distance between them. Behind her, she heard the heavy footsteps of his men as they moved toward the other Huey to retrieve the boxes of bottled water and carry them to the distribution center.

As Kerry drew closer to Quinn, her heart soared unexpectedly with such a rush of overwhelming happiness that it shook her completely. The Marine had an oval face with a rock hard-looking chin. Though his lips were thinned, she could see he had a wide mouth, with laugh lines deeply indented at each corner. His nose was long and straight, the nostrils flaring as she approached, as if to pick up her scent. He was more wild animal than human to her and yet despite the quality of danger surrounding Grayson, his presence made her feel secure for the first time since the quake. This Marine knew how to protect, she could feel it in her bones. His black brows were straight across his large, glittering blue eyes. The color of his eyes reminded Kerry of the glacial ice up in Alaska. His pupils were large and black, and she saw intelligence gleaming in his gaze, as well as alertness and surprise. Why the surprise, she wondered as she lifted her hand to wave, her mouth pulling into a relieved smile.

"Corporal Grayson? I'm Kerry Chelton. Welcome to our little corner of the world."

As he made the trip over to area five, Quinn had decided to keep things on a business level and not be very friendly. Now, as the tall, willowy woman in the sheriff's deputy uniform held out her hand toward him, he felt his resolve falter. The photo he'd seen of Kerry Chelton had done nothing to prepare him for the woman before him now. Short brown hair rife with gold highlights framed her heart-shaped face. Maybe it was the look of relief in her huge gray eyes that reached inside his hardened heart. Or maybe it was the way the corners of her mouth softened and her lower lip trembled as she welcomed him.

Or maybe he was just damn attracted to this woman who he had been assigned to work with from dawn till dusk....

* * * * *

**Where royalty and romance
go hand in hand...**

The series finishes in

with these unforgettable love stories:

THE ROYAL TREATMENT
by Maureen Child
October 2002 (SD #1468)

TAMING THE PRINCE
by Elizabeth Bevarly
November 2002 (SD #1474)

ROYALLY PREGNANT
by Barbara McCauley
December 2002 (SD #1480)

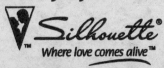

magazine

♥────────────────────────── **quizzes**

Is he the one? What kind of lover are you? Visit the **Quizzes** area to find out!

♥────────────────────── **recipes for romance**

Get scrumptious meal ideas with our **Recipes for Romance.**

♥────────────────────── **romantic movies**

Peek at the **Romantic Movies** area to find Top 10 Flicks about First Love, ten Supersexy Movies, and more.

♥────────────────────────── **royal romance**

Get the latest scoop on your favorite royals in **Royal Romance.**

♥──────────────────────────────── **games**

Check out the **Games** pages to find a ton of interactive romantic fun!

♥────────────────────── **romantic travel**

In need of a romantic rendezvous? Visit the **Romantic Travel** section for articles and guides.

♥──────────────────────────── **lovescopes**

Are you two compatible? Click your way to the **Lovescopes** area to find out now!

Silhouette —

where love comes alive—online...

Visit us online at
www.eHarlequin.com

Silhouette *Desire*

presents

DYNASTIES:
THE
CONNELLYS

A brand-new miniseries about the Connellys of Chicago,
a wealthy, powerful American family tied by blood to the
royal family of the island kingdom of Altaria.
They're wealthy, powerful and rocked by
scandal, betrayal…and passion!

Look for a whole year of glamorous and
utterly romantic tales in 2002:

Silhouette®

Where love comes alive™

Visit Silhouette at www.eHarlequin.com

SDDYN02

October 2002
TAMING THE OUTLAW
#1465 by Cindy Gerard

Don't miss bestselling author
Cindy Gerard's exciting story about
a sexy cowboy's reunion with his
old flame—and the daughter he
didn't know he had!

November 2002
ALL IN THE GAME
#1471 by Barbara Boswell

In the latest tale by beloved
Desire author Barbara Boswell,
a feisty beauty joins her twin as a
reality game show contestant in an
island paradise…and comes face-to-
face with her teenage crush!

December 2002
A COWBOY & A GENTLEMAN
#1477 by Ann Major

Sparks fly when two fiery Texans are
brought together by matchmaking
relatives, in this dynamic story by
the ever-popular Ann Major.

MAN OF THE MONTH

Some men are made for lovin'—and you're sure to love
these three upcoming men of the month!

Available at your favorite retail outlet.

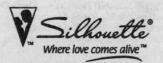

Where love comes alive™

COMING NEXT MONTH

#1465 TAMING THE OUTLAW—Cindy Gerard
After six years, sexy Cutter Reno was back in town and wreaking havoc on Peg Lathrop's emotions. Peg still yearned passionately for Cutter—and he wanted to pick up where they had left off. But would he still want her once he learned her precious secret?

**#1466 CINDERELLA'S CONVENIENT HUSBAND—
Katherine Garbera**
Dynasties: The Connellys
Lynn McCoy would do anything to keep the ranch that had been in her family for generations—even marry wealthy Seth Connelly. And when she fell in love with him, Lynn needed to convince her handsome husband they could have their very own happily-ever-after.

#1467 THE SEAL's SURPRISE BABY—Amy J. Fetzer
A trip home turned Jack Singer's life upside down because he learned that beautiful Melanie Patterson, with whom he'd spent one unforgettable night, had secretly borne him a daughter. The honor-bound Navy SEAL proposed a marriage of convenience. But Melanie refused, saying she didn't want him to feel obligated to her. Could Jack persuade her he wanted to be a *real* father…and husband?

#1468 THE ROYAL TREATMENT—Maureen Child
Crown and Glory
Determined to get an interview with the royal family, anchorwoman Jade Erickson went to the palace—and found herself trapped in an elevator in the arms of the handsomest man she'd ever seen. Jeremy Wainwright made her heart beat faster, and he was equally attracted to her, but would the flame of their unexpected passion continue to burn red-hot?

#1469 HEARTS ARE WILD—Laura Wright
Maggie Connor got more than she'd bargained for when she vowed to find the perfect woman for her very attractive male roommate. Nick Kaplan was turning out to be everything *she'd* ever wanted in a man, and she was soon yearning to keep him for herself!

#1470 SECRETS, LIES…AND PASSION—Linda Conrad
An old flame roared back to life when FBI agent Reid Sorrels returned to his hometown to track a suspect. His former fiancée, Jill Bennett, was as lovely as ever, and the electricity between them was undeniable. But they both had secrets.…